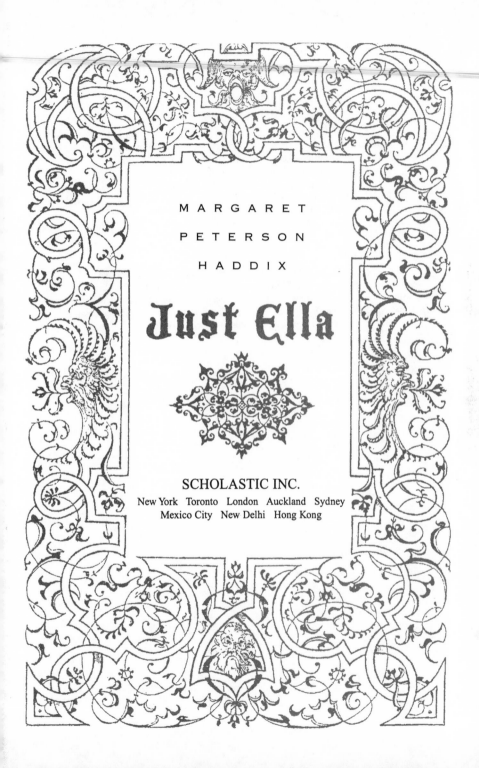

MARGARET

PETERSON

HADDIX

Just Ella

SCHOLASTIC INC.

New York   Toronto   London   Auckland   Sydney
Mexico City   New Delhi   Hong Kong

ISBN 0-439-29690-0

12 11 10 9 8 7 6 5 4 3   1 2 3 4 5 6/0

Printed in the U.S.A.   37

First Scholastic printing, February 2001

FOR

Meredith, Faith, Kristen, and Sarah

Just Ella

1

The fire had gone out, and I didn't know what to do.

I was covered with a king's ransom of silk-sewn comforters and surrounded by six warming pans, so I was still mostly warm. But my nose was exposed and freezing, and I heard no friendly crackling from the direction of the hearth. For some reason the chambermaid in charge of keeping my fire going had overslept or forgotten me. Or perhaps I had awakened too early, before it was time for her to come on duty. I hadn't figured out the palace work schedule yet.

The last time I awoke to freezing air and a dead fire, I simply got up and restarted it myself. "Ella," I lectured myself, "you're no stranger to tending fireplaces. Just because they put a crown on your head doesn't mean your hands forgot how to work." Still, I had to force myself to leave the bed's warmth, tiptoe across the icy flagstones, and search for a tinderbox and poker.

For a while I feared none of that was in my room—did they think princesses or almost-princesses were too delicate even to see the instruments that kept them warm? But then I found a compartment in the wall by the great fireplace and dragged out equipment bigger and grander than I'd ever used before. Reviving the fire was a struggle, for my hands were clumsy after two weeks of idleness. (I hardly count needlepoint as work.)

At the end, when I was finally able to warm my numb fingers over ever-growing flames, I felt a strange surge of pride. I wanted to brag to someone about accomplishing a chore I'd done hundreds of times in my old life without thinking. But there was no one to tell. Charm wouldn't be interested, even if I saw him, in between his endless hunts and contests. The king was even more remote, and I'd endured enough blank stares from the queen to know I shouldn't confide anything in her. Then there were all my ladies-in-waiting and maidservants and my instructors (one for decorum, one for dancing, one for palace protocol, one for needlepoint, one for painting, and two or three whose purposes I had yet to figure out). But all of them looked at me with such horror whenever I let something slip about my former life. ("What? You had no one to do your laundry?" one of the silliest of my waiting girls, Simprianna, had asked when I'd carelessly mentioned rinsing out my stockings after the ball.) Even after just two weeks, I knew better than to brag to anyone in the castle about doing something that dirtied my hands.

And so I thought I'd keep my fire-building secret. Then

I overheard two of my maidservants gossiping later that day about my chambermaid.

"She was found still in her bed, and it was already past five o'clock," the one said to the other, fluffing my pillows with a dainty thump. (In the castle, even the maids pretend to be dainty.)

"No," the other gasped. "So she was—"

"Beaten within an inch of her life and dismissed," the first said, sounding as self-satisfied as rabble cheering an execution. "Thrown out the palace gate by six."

"Lazy slugabed got exactly what she deserved, then," the second said, even as she gently placed a single rose on my pillow. "But the fire—"

They both fell silent and glanced my way. I lowered my eyes and pretended to be intent on the watercolor I was copying over in the afternoon light struggling through the western window. I don't know why I cared what maids thought, or why I acted as though restarting a fire to heat my own room was something to be ashamed of. After a moment, one said, "Humph," and the other echoed her, and they left. I sighed, glad to be alone, but then Madame Bisset, my decorum instructor, arrived in a flurry.

If it had been someone else, I would have said she was disheveled and flustered, but, of course, Madame Bisset never allowed herself to be anything but absolutely perfect in bearing and dress. Every gleaming silver hair was in place, every one of the fifty-two tiny mother-of-pearl buttons that marched up her dress was precisely fastened in its loop. But she looked as though she'd given thought to appearing disheveled, as though circumstances might warrant it from anyone else.

"Princess Cynthiana Eleanora," she said sternly as she sat down, discreetly arranging the yards and yards of fabric in her skirt so she would be comfortable on the sofa. "I have heard a rumor."

The unfamiliar name and title jarred, as always. I had only recently managed to stop myself from looking around when people addressed me like that. A princess? Where? Oh, that's right. Me. Sort of.

"Madame? A rumor?" I murmured, trying to get the pronunciation of "Madame" exactly right. The day before, Madame Bisset had chided me for how—she lowered her voice to whisper the horrifying phrase—"common" my French sounded. This "Madame" evidently passed muster, because Madame Bisset's frown didn't deepen immediately. So I worried instead that I was breaking some rule against echoing another speaker's words. But no, it was my father who had opposed that. I could hear his dry voice: "I'd prefer to hear an original thought, if you have one." I couldn't imagine Madame Bisset caring about my thoughts, original or otherwise.

"A rumor," she said firmly. "Now, normally, a cultured woman does not listen to rumors or gossip. *Au contraire,* one must hold oneself above such—such crudity. But this rumor is so appalling, it must be dealt with. And since I am the person responsible for instilling you with a sense of etiquette, I must not shirk."

She sniffed daintily and dramatically, fully conveying

both her dedication to her responsibilities and her distaste for the subject she was about to discuss. In my first few days in the palace, when I still dared, I would have joked, "You mean, it's a dirty job, but somebody's got to do it?" But I'd learned.

"Now, the servants are saying—" Her inflection on "servants" carried the full weight of her disgust at being put in a position of having to quote servants. "The servants are saying you lit your own fire this morning."

"I did," I said in a small voice.

Madame Bisset gasped and went pale. She leaned back against the sofa. I wondered if I was going to have to call for smelling salts.

"You must never do that again," she said in a surprisingly firm voice. "Never."

A proper young lady would have bowed her head in shame and murmured, "Yes, Madame Bisset." But no one had thought of training me to be proper until two weeks earlier, so my instincts were all wrong.

"Why?" I asked, truly curious.

Madame Bisset gasped again, as if I were beyond hope if I had to ask. She took a deep breath—as deep as her corsets allowed, anyway.

"You have no idea why you should not light your own fire."

It was a question without being a question—a trick. I'd be rude to answer it, perhaps interrupting her next thought. But I'd be more rude not to answer, if she was waiting for a reply. These were the games I had to play now.

"No," I ventured. "Or—I'm not really as stupid as you think. I mean, I know princesses usually don't do things like that. But I was cold, and—"

"You were cold," Madame Bisset said. A lesser woman would have rolled her eyes. Not Madame Bisset, of course, but the muscles around her eyelids twitched ever so slightly, as if they knew what was possible. "You were cold. Did you perchance remember that you have a bell to call your servants? Did you remember that it was *their* job to tend your fire?"

"Yes, but—" I looked down, knowing that if I kept looking at Madame Bisset, she'd see that I suddenly wanted to cry. I almost whispered, "But I didn't want to disturb anyone."

I looked up in time to see Madame Bisset holding back an explosion. The color in her face rose like a thermometer, first deathly white, then fiery red, clear up to the roots of her curled-back hair.

"You must never, ever hesitate to disturb a servant," she said, shooting off each word like an arrow, precise and cruel. "That's what they're there for. They exist solely to serve us."

She closed her eyes, then opened them slowly.

"You may think you're being kind," she said, the strain of trying to sound understanding weighing in her voice. "But servants know their place. They like to serve. They are hurt if you make them feel useless. Purposeless. And they cannot respect a member of the nobility who lowers herself to their level, to their *work*."

She said "work" like it was a curse word.

I clenched my teeth—an ugly habit, I'd been told again and again. But if I opened my mouth, I knew the angry words would spill out. What did Madame Bisset know about how servants felt and thought? Why did she think anyone would get any pleasure out of serving lazy, selfish, self-centered people like her? I knew. I'd been there—not a servant, quite, but close enough. I'd had no respect for the ones I waited on, to begin with. If they'd so much as raised a finger to help me, the question was, would I have been able to stop hating them?

"Do you understand?" Madame Bisset asked, the way you'd ask a simpleton.

I lowered my eyes and made a stab at propriety.

"Yes, Madame Bisset." I looked up, unable to resist another question. "The maidservant—I heard she was dismissed. If I'd thought to ring for her, would she still have been—"

Madame Bisset sniffed.

"Of course. She overslept."

So now, cold again, I dared not get up. I couldn't start my own fire or ring for the maid, and risk getting another girl fired. I could only pray that she woke on her own, and crept down here without being discovered. I willed her to awaken, as if I could send my thoughts up three flights of narrow, winding stairs to shake her awake. I listened for the distinctive creak of my door, the one I so often pretended to sleep through, because I didn't know what to say to people doing work for me that I was perfectly capable of doing myself. But the door didn't open. I got colder.

This wasn't what I'd imagined at the ball, the stars wheeling above me as I danced with the prince. Truthfully, I didn't imagine anything. Just being at the ball was beyond my wildest dreams. And then everything happened so fast—the prince seeking me for his bended-knee proposal, everyone making wedding plans, me returning to the castle to stay, for good. I remembered an old neighbor woman cackling as I rode by, astonished, in the prince's carriage: "Now, there's one who will live happily ever after."

I was cold. I was lonely. I was engaged to be married in two short months to the most handsome man I'd ever seen—the prince of the land, the heir to the throne. But I had never felt so alone in all my life, not even shivering in rags in my garret the day they came to say my father was dead.

This was happiness?

2

I must have fallen back asleep, because when I opened my eyes again, there was a weak fire throwing shadows on the wall. Sunlight streamed in through the one high, narrow window, doing its best to brighten the dark room. I hadn't known this, having stepped foot in a castle only once before I came to stay for good, but castles are dim, gloomy places, full of shadows even at noon on the brightest day. My eyes had not adjusted. As a child, I had lived more out of doors than in, until my father taught me to read just to keep me in the house. And even then, I'd sneak his books outside and read them under the shade of the hazel tree, or while dangling my bare feet in the creek behind our house.

And now, I hadn't been outside the castle walls once since I arrived. Aren't princesses supposed to know horsemanship or anything like that? Shouldn't someone be giving me some sort of lessons outside? I resolved to ask. The thought cheered me so much, I sprang out of bed and began scrubbing my face with vigor.

Four hours later I was on my third lesson of the morning, and I still hadn't found an opportunity to ask anything. How could conversational French, dining table
etiquette, and royal genealogy take so much time? Actually, royal genealogy would have interested me if it had
been the kind my father used to talk about, where kings
went crazy or a single peasant's whisper in a prince's ear
changed the entire fate of a nation. In the history Lord
Reston described for me, in his dry, dull, droning voice,
everyone was upstanding and perfect, and absolutely
nothing of interest ever happened.

"And then the next king, Charming the Ninth, was
known as the Bridges King, because he ordered the building of thousands of bridges throughout the land. And
every bridge was strong and true and lasted for hundreds
of years," he said, his hands resting on his enormous
stomach. He looked like a huge pig stuffed into men's
clothing. I thought of warning him never to go to the Hay-
market Fair held in our village every summer, because
boys there put clothes and wigs on pigs and chase them
for sport, and he wouldn't want to be mistaken for a particularly well-dressed pig. I'd hate to think of Lord Reston
trying to run.

"Some of the bridges exist even to this—"

Lord Reston's drone stopped abruptly. He gasped
soundlessly, a stricken look on his face.

"Lord Reston? Are you all right?" I asked. "Lord Reston?"

His head lolled to the side, his tongue hanging out of
his mouth. His face went gray.

"Lord Reston? Lord Reston?" Frantically I pawed at his collar hidden beneath rolls of double chins. I popped off his top button and undid his cravat. He had to get air. Why wasn't he breathing? "Help! Somebody help!" I screamed.

The castle walls were too thick for anyone to hear me unless they were right outside the door. Nobody came. I tugged and pulled on Lord Reston's arms and legs, thinking that if I could get him flat on the floor, perhaps the air would come in more easily. Even after my years of carrying buckets and firewood, moving him took every ounce of my strength. Finally he fell from the chair with a thud. I straightened his body out, trying to make him more comfortable. I thought I saw his chest moving up and down, ever so slightly, but I didn't stop to make sure.

"I'll be right back, Lord Reston," I shouted over my shoulder as I raced for help. "I promise."

Out in the hall, I lifted my skirts to run. There had to be maids about in the next chamber, or the next, and one of them could go for a physician. If only I could find one who knew or cared enough to run as fast as she could. Turning the corner, I collided with a serving girl, a child really, no more than ten or eleven.

"Go get the court physician!" I commanded. "Tell him Lord Reston is dying in my room!"

"Yes, Princess," she said, sweeping into a graceful curtsy.

"There's no time for that! Run!" I commanded.

Obediently, she stopped mid-curtsy and fled.

I rushed back to my room, praying I wouldn't find Lord Reston already dead. A stench told me he was still alive enough to have fouled himself. I knelt beside him.

"Lord Reston? Can you hear me?" I took his cold hand in mine, wishing I hadn't been so cruel as to think of him as a pig. He may have been pompous and dull, but surely he had a family, people who loved him. . . .

"Unhhh," he grunted.

"That's good," I said encouragingly. "I'm glad you're in there. But don't try to talk if it hurts."

I bent over him, putting my ear on his chest to listen for his heartbeat. It was there, but faint and sluggish, as if his heart were not quite sure the next *thump-thump* was worth the effort.

"Princess! Whatever are you doing?"

I turned, and there was Madame Bisset, arriving for my next lesson.

"It's Lord Reston—he's taken ill. Do you know anything about—"

I stopped because Madame Bisset was looking at me in such horror. She'd gone white.

"It's *His Excellency,* the Lord Reston," she corrected.

I hardly thought a title mattered under the circumstances.

"And a true princess," she continued, pronouncing each word with great effort, "would never lie on the floor with her head on a man's chest—a man's bare chest."

She swayed ever so slightly, prepared to faint.

I looked down and saw that Lord Reston's shirt was

open practically to his waist, his immense girth spilling out. Hastily I tried to pull his waistcoat together, but the effort was in vain. I scrambled up and helped Madame Bisset to the chaise longue.

"I'm afraid he's dying," I said. "I didn't know what to do—"

"That's what doctors are for," Madame Bisset said weakly, her eyes closed.

"Yes, I sent for one," I said irritably. I glanced over at Lord Reston, who probably was dying as we spoke. "But there wasn't a doctor here when he was stricken. Just me."

Madame Bisset's only response was to flutter her eyelashes.

Just then the court physician swept into the room. He was a spry little man I'd glimpsed only from a distance at formal court functions. He had an entourage of several men, all respectfully standing several steps back.

He bowed deeply before even glancing at Lord Reston's body on the floor.

"Princess, Madame, charmed as ever," he said. "Now, I must beg you to excuse us."

It took me a minute to realize he meant for us to leave. Madame Bisset, suddenly energized, rose quickly and gave me a stern look that made me feel like a dog being commanded to heel. I followed her out the door.

"We will use my chambers for your lesson today," she said calmly, as if Lord Reston's collapse were not worth mentioning when I still had so much to learn about the proper ways to address various visiting dignitaries.

"They'll tell us how he is, won't they?" I asked. I had to walk quickly to keep up with her. But she was gliding as smoothly as if she had wheels instead of legs, and I was bouncing up and down and half tripping on the layers of my dress. I longed to hike up the skirt again, as I had while running for help. But I knew that would make Madame Bisset faint for real.

"I hadn't realized you were so fond of His Excellency," she said drily. "I'm sure you'll be told whatever's appropriate."

That word, *appropriate,* took a minute to sink in. *No,* I wanted to shout, *I want to be told whatever's true.* But I didn't.

"Yes, Madame Bisset," I said meekly.

3

I sat through the rest of the morning's lessons in a daze, paying even less attention than usual to Madame Siles, the needlepoint instructor, and Lord Axley, who was trying to teach me proper ways of dealing with servants. (His lessons had been added only after the fireplace fiasco.) At the noon meal with my ladies-in-waiting, I barely noticed the conversation, which was a silly stream of chatter about who had what color ribbons in their hair and why. I was pondering an experiment.

If I didn't ask, how long would it be before anyone told me how Lord Reston was?

And would anybody ever say to me, "Gosh, that must have been awful for you, seeing him collapse like that; if that ever happens again, here's how you can help . . ."?

I didn't think so.

I dunked an edge of bread into my soup. The bread was made of the finest-ground white flour in the kingdom, and it was served only in the castle. The luxury was lost on me—it seemed tasteless compared with the coarse brown bread Mrs. Branson made back in my village and had sometimes shared with me if there was any left over after her husband and ten children ate. My mouth watered at the memory. Maybe once my place in the castle was a little more established—once I wasn't being chastised for trying to save a man's life—maybe I could convince whoever controlled such things to make Mrs. Branson an extra royal baker. The Bransons could certainly use the money, though Lucille, my stepmother, would be outraged that I was helping the Bransons and not her or my stepsisters. I imagined saying to any of the Step-Evils, "Hey, if you want to bake bread, that's great. But I thought none of you were into that, seeing as how you always made me do all the work."

As usual, thinking about the Step-Evils made me feel uncomfortable and guilty and angry all at once. On that dizzying day when Prince Charming found me, when it was clear the glass slipper was mine and he was going to whisk me off to the palace, Lucille had suddenly turned into my best friend, hugging me and going on and on about how she couldn't be happier if it were one of her *real* daughters becoming a princess, and how she knew, from all our heart-to-heart talks, that this was my dearest wish, but wouldn't it be nice if my dear, dear mother and sisters could come to the castle with me?

"Stepmother," I'd corrected quietly. "Stepsisters."

One of the things that had endeared the prince to me forever was that he'd looked at the pile of rags that I'd cast off and then looked at Lucille and Griselda and Corimunde in their tacky, expensive finery, and shut the door of the coach right in Lucille's face. I hadn't seen any of the Step-Evils since. Should I? Should I, for example, ask that they be invited to the wedding?

I was so lost in thought that it took me a long time to realize everyone else at the table had suddenly stopped talking and was staring in horror at me. Was I accidentally speaking my thoughts aloud, raving like the village lunatic? Had I sprouted green hair on my face?

"Princess," the lady-in-waiting to my right hissed, and pointed with a severe tilt of her chin.

Behind me, a servant girl darted in to wipe up the single drop of soup that had fallen from my bread to the tablecloth. Madame Bisset, seated catty-corner and five seats down, rose and came to whisper in my ear, "Only commoners place their bread into the soup. You must never, never do that again."

"All right," I said with a jauntiness I didn't feel. "I'll be certain to remember that."

Everyone returned to their soup again, bowing their heads so they didn't have to look at me. A dozen spoons moved in unison, dipping out of the bowls backward so as not to drip, exactly the way Lady Wesley had tried to teach me.

Somehow I didn't think my idea of brown bread at the castle would go over very well. Would I spend the rest of my life pretending to like white bread? Pretending a drop of soup on the tablecloth was a disastrous turn of events?

Pretending I was more interested in colored ribbons than in anything else?

"So," I said, a bit too loudly, "has anyone heard how His Excellency, the Lord Reston is doing?" I was proud I'd remembered to say his full title. Surely Madame Bisset couldn't criticize me now.

A flurry of whispers circled the table.

"I believe," Madame Bisset said calmly, "he is resting and doing well. He was taken ill during Princess Cynthiana Eleanora's lesson this morning," she explained to the several ladies who were staring from me to her with puzzled expressions.

Ill? I wanted to say. *He was—apoplectic. He almost died in front of me.*

The other girls and women were shifting uncomfortably in their seats. If they hadn't all been so refined, I would have said they were squirming.

"Why does this bother everyone so much?" I asked. "I mean, I could understand you being concerned about Lord Reston's health. But none of you even want to speak of this. Why?"

Madame Bisset took it upon herself to speak for everyone.

"His *Excellency's* illness is of a particularly unpleasant nature," she said. "As you must know, our duty as women is to be protected from unpleasantness, so that our minds and our souls—and our brows—shall be unsullied by worry. Women were created to be like flowers, providing color and beauty to the world. We leave troubling matters to men."

The other women were nodding and murmuring assent.

"Oh, Madame Bisset, you express yourself so beautifully," the lady beside me said.

I considered suggesting that Madame Bisset ask the female servants in the palace if they believed they were protected from unpleasantness. I thought of the response she'd get if she tried out her theory on the women I knew back in the village, who worked from sunup until sundown scrubbing and baking and wiping snotty noses.

"Surely you understand now," Madame Bisset asked.

I didn't say yes or no, but let the conversation meander back to ribbons.

4

A long, dull afternoon of needlepoint stretched ahead of me, so I dawdled leaving the dining room. That meant I was alone when I felt a timid tug on my dress.

"Please, miss. I mean, Princess."

It was the child I'd sent for the doctor.

"Me mum, she's the one tending to that lord now, she says he's got a fair to middling chance of making it, and if he pulls through the night, he could live another twenty years. Except nobody knows if he'll ever be really himself again, because he can't move one of his arms and one of his legs, and half his face don't move neither. But"—the last words came out in a rush—"me mum says he wouldn't be alive at all if you hadn't sent for help so quick and made sure he could breathe and all."

The child stood back on her heels, looking at me doubtfully, as if afraid I might punish her for speaking.

"Thank you," I said. "I hope somebody else

thanked you too, for running for help so quickly. You're really the one who saved Lord Reston's life."

The girl hunched her shoulders modestly.

"That's what me mum says."

I felt the familiar stab of envy, hearing someone talk about a mother who obviously loved her. My own mother had died when I was born, and my father said it hurt to talk about her, so I had very little in the way of even secondhand memories. Certainly Lucille was no substitute for a loving mother. And I'd lost my father, too.

I dragged myself out of self-pity and directed my attention back to the child. Her dirt-colored hair was cut in a ragged circle around her face, and her cheeks and hands were so grubby it was hard to tell how long ago they'd been washed, if ever. And anyhow, her nose was too big and her mouth was too small—no one could mistake her purpose in life to be providing beauty. But her eyes were lively and quick, and I found myself looking at them and forgetting the rest.

"What's your name, child?" I asked.

"Mary."

"I'm—well, I guess you know who I am," I said. "How about if we make a deal. If you get a chance, could you let me know tomorrow how Lord Reston is doing? You're the first person who's been honest with me. I don't have anything with me now, but I'm sure I can come up with some reward for you."

Mary giggled.

"Oh, that don't matter. I just thought you'd want to know. I heard you ask at the table. Don't that Madame Bisset beat all?"

Mary's pronunciation of "Madame" was actually better and more French sounding than mine. She probably knew more about palace protocol too. I squinted thoughtfully. Mary wasn't more than four or five years younger than me. It didn't seem fair that I was now a princess and she would always be a servant, just because I looked a little prettier than her.

"Madame Bisset does beat all," I agreed. "You won't get in trouble for talking to me, will you?"

"Are you kidding?" Mary said. "Not as long as you don't mind."

"All right, then—," I started, when someone called from down the corridor, "Princess—"

"See you tomorrow," I told Mary.

I went off to my needlepoint feeling a little cheerier.

That evening was my time to meet with the prince. We had an hour together just about every other night, depending on his schedule. I saw him at the banquet table every night, of course, but that was often from a distance, because the seating chart always changed. In the beginning, they always placed me with Madame Bisset and my other instructors, so they could correct any horrifying error I made before it attracted too much attention. I could tell someone thought I was learning something, because in the last few days I'd occasionally gotten to sit near people who hadn't heard anything but the castle's official story—that I was a foreign princess who'd disguised herself as a commoner, because I wanted to win Prince Charming's love on my own merits, not because of my father's vast lands. I thought anyone who believed the castle's official story had to be several logs short of a roaring fire, but nobody asked me.

Now I sat in the prince's vast antechamber, waiting. The protocol of these visits was strictly regimented. Someone—usually one of my older and therefore more mature ladies-in-waiting—had to walk me down the hall and make sure there was a chaperon in attendance. My lady-in-waiting would curtsy and discreetly remove herself. Then the door to the prince's bedchambers, a place I'd never seen, would open, and I'd catch my breath and try to make conversation with the prince, the man I was going to marry.

I studied the tapestry on the wall, a dramatic scene of huntsmen killing a wild boar. There were dogs yapping at the boar, blood pouring from his sides, a nobleman with a sword poised above him, ready to deliver the final thrust. Women must have stitched this gory scene—needlepoint wasn't for men. How did that fit with Madame Bisset's notion that women must be protected from all unpleasantness? I dismissed her ideas as too silly to even think about.

Behind me, tonight's chaperon, an ancient retainer of the king's, snuffled. He sounded like he had a bad cold. The candles sputtered in their sconces. The old grandfather clock by the door donged eight times. Not twelve—not midnight, the hour I had dreaded and run from on the most exciting evening of my entire life . . .

Remembering the ball, I almost missed the opening door. But then there was the prince, in all his glory: clear blue eyes, high cheekbones, rugged jaw, blond hair precisely the right length because it was cut every fourth day by the royal barber. Tonight the prince was wearing a deep blue waistcoat that exactly matched his eyes and showed off his muscular chest and trim waist. My heart quickened, as always. Dizzily, I thought back to a summer afternoon years ago, before the Step-Evils entered my life, when several of the other girls in the neighborhood and I were wading in the creek behind our house, talking of whom we would marry.

"This is posh," Vena, a gloomy girl none of us really liked, had muttered. "We'll all settle for whoever asks us. We'll just be lucky if we don't get someone like my dad."

Her father was a well-known ne'er-do-well, who spent most of his time in the village tavern.

"Not me," I said. "I won't settle. If the right person doesn't ask, I won't marry at all."

Some of the girls gasped, I remember. What would they have said if I'd vowed to marry a prince?

Now I murmured, "Your Majesty," trying to sound properly dignified and feminine and loving. I bent forward and extended my hand for kissing. Charm took it, and the brush of his lips on my skin sent shivers down my spine.

"Princess," he said.

His voice was low and deep, just as you would expect. Perfect, like everything else about him.

He sat down beside me, his left leg a scant inch from my skirt.

"Have you had a good day?" I asked.

"Yes," he said. "And you?"

I hesitated. Had he heard about Lord Reston? Would I be violating some etiquette rule by bringing up his condition? I didn't know if Prince Charming realized that Lord Reston was tutoring me, or if Prince Charming even knew who Lord Reston was. No wonder I kept making so many gaffes—I never thought to ask the important questions until it was too late. Tonight, I decided, the less said the better.

"My day was fine, Your Majesty," I murmured.

"Good," he said.

The chaperon coughed behind us. The clock ticked. I saw the time on its face: 8:03. And already Prince Charming and I had run out of things to say.

I often wished, during these stiff meetings, that I could skip ahead in my life, past the glorious wedding, to maybe a year from now. Then, after many hours together without a chaperon, I could picture the prince and me cuddling cozily on these cushions instead of sitting stiffly an inch apart. We'd share our deepest thoughts and dreams, forgetting there was a castle or a kingdom or anything outside our love for each other. We'd call each other Charm and El, not "Majesty" and "Princess."

So far I'd called Prince Charming "Charm" only in my mind.

Prince Charming gave me an innocent, adorable smile.

He didn't seem to realize that the chaperon made me feel awkward, or that the silence between us was uncomfortable and unnatural.

Charm and I hadn't talked much the night of the ball either, but then, we didn't need to. When we danced, he kept one hand on just the right spot on the small of my back, gently guiding me. His other hand held mine. We looked into each other's eyes, and it seemed like he already knew everything about me. He didn't let me dance with anyone else. He whispered in my ear, "You're the most beautiful girl here."

Hey, I was as susceptible to flattery as the next girl.

Sometimes he still told me I was beautiful, but it wasn't like he was really paying attention.

"What are you thinking about?" I asked.

He jerked his head toward me, jolted by the urgency in my voice.

"The hunt," he said, then looked puzzled. I may have surprised him into telling the truth.

"You went hunting today," I said, trying to coax more out of him. "Did you catch much?"

The word *catch* sounded odd. Back home we used to talk about catching fish. That's what I was thinking of. But the deer and wild boars and other animals worthy of royalty's attention weren't "caught." Should I have said "killed"? Were ladies allowed to say that? How could Prince Charming and I ever talk the way I wanted to—no holds barred, our thoughts as close as our bodies had been at the grand ball—if we couldn't even use the same words?

The prince smiled indulgently.

"Don't trouble your mind about that," he said. "The kingdom is in fine shape. Why, we throw away food here at the castle that would be a feast in Suala."

Suala was a neighboring kingdom. We had been at war with Suala for as long as I could remember, so maybe the prince was only showing bravado, the way street urchins brag about the number of maggots in the bread they steal. But still, I wondered. . . .

"Why?" I asked. "Why throw away food when some of your own subjects go hungry each night? Why, I myself know—"

The prince toyed with a ringlet that had escaped from the ribbon holding my hair in place. He wrapped and unwrapped my long blond curl around his fingers. I wished my hair had feeling. I wished he were touching my hand instead. I couldn't remember what I was going to say I knew.

The prince chuckled.

"So my princess worries about the poor," he said. "If it pleases you, I'll order that our table scraps be set outside the palace gate each evening."

"It's that easy?" I asked. "Just like that?"

The prince shrugged.

"Why not? It matters not to me."

He smiled and I should have smiled back, given him the gratitude he deserved. But his last words stopped me.

Why didn't his own hungry subjects matter to him? What was wrong with this man?

5

The next morning, when the time came that I normally met with Lord Reston, I sat wondering if someone else would replace him or if—miracle of miracles—I'd actually have some time to myself. I was irritated that, once again, nobody had told me anything. The servants all knew my schedule—how else did the maids know exactly when to flounce in to make my bed, exactly when to make themselves scarce? But I, the supposed princess, never knew from one minute to the next what I was supposed to do or where I was supposed to be until someone hissed last-minute instructions to me. Probably the little servant girl, Mary, could have told me yesterday who was going to take over teaching whatever it was Lord Reston was supposed to be teaching me.

I had just decided that if I did have a free moment, I'd like to hunt Mary up to check on Lord Reston, when a strange knock sounded at my door. I say strange, because until that moment, I'd never thought about the fact that every single person in the castle knocked in one of two ways. All the servants knocked once loudly, as if to guarantee they got my attention, and then once softly, as if to apologize that their humble selves were so disrespectful as to disturb royalty. Everyone else, all my instructors and the ladies-in-waiting and other nobility, knocked four times, emphatically, the knocks as good as saying, "I am important!" and "Acknowledge me at once!"

But this knock was like a half line of music: *Duuunh-duh da da da*. Without thinking, I went to the door and gave the two answering knocks it seemed to demand. *Duh duh*. Then I pushed open the door.

A young man I'd never seen before stood in the corridor. He was perhaps a half decade older than me, tall, and much too thin for his frame and his clothes. The clothes also seemed too formal for his comfort somehow, although by castle standards they were practically slovenly: dark velvet breeches with worn knees, a wrinkled white shirt, a brown coat and waistcoat of obviously good wool, but poorly sewn. His dark curly hair could most charitably be called mussed; it reminded me of the way our village had looked after a windstorm toppled three houses and knocked down six trees.

The man's muddy brown eyes were as wide open and stunned-looking as if he'd just personally witnessed such a storm.

"Yes?" I said.

"Princess—I had no idea—I mean . . . I don't mean to be forward, but you're even more beautiful up close," he stammered.

I sighed. I hated this reaction. About the time I passed my thirteenth summer, two years ago, men had begun looking at me strangely. The butcher's boy, whom I had previously considered a sensible fellow, followed me around for five days with an expression as addlepated as a cow off her feed. He got in the way when I tried to scrub every flagstone of our front path by hand, the way Lucille demanded. I finally had to tell him I'd pull every one of his fingernails out with my bare hands if he didn't leave me alone. (I wouldn't—and couldn't—have done it, of course, but he was too stupid and lovesick to know that.) That got rid of him, but I still hated to go to the butcher's because of him. Or I did, before I became a princess and didn't have to sort through animal entrails anymore.

Of course, if I'd bothered pondering it, I would have thought becoming a princess and wearing fancy dresses instead of rags—and having several maids whose sole purpose in life seemed to be making me beautiful— would have subjected me to more addlepated expressions than ever. But it hadn't. Maybe being the prince's betrothed was as good as wearing a sign that said; "Addle or pate over this girl, and the prince could have you beheaded." Before this young man—or boy, really, he wasn't much more than a boy—every glance directed my way had been perfectly discreet and bland. But he was still gawking.

"Well," I said, "thank you. But please, I beg you, don't let it bother you."

He shut his gaping mouth and gave a little jerk and returned to what I guessed must be normal for him. He dipped into an awkward bow, almost laughably off balance, then swung back up sideways and introduced himself.

"I'm Jed Reston. I'm sure someone told you—I'm going to be teaching you because my father is . . . er, dang it, I'm not used to talking to princesses. What words am I allowed to use to tell you what happened to my father?"

I stepped aside to let him into the room.

"I'm not really a princess," I said, forgetting myself. Then I quickly added, "I mean, I wasn't raised the way a princess would be raised in this kingdom. And I saw what happened to your father. How is he now?"

"Just fine. Thank you for your concern." The words came out rapid-fire, like blasts from several cannons at once.

"No, *really*," I said. "Tell me. I don't care what words you use."

Jed grimaced.

"Still mostly paralyzed. But you can tell that underneath, he's furious at not being able to get up and walk and talk and act pompous. Oops. Dang it again. Dad's right. I never will learn to be diplomatic."

He looked so nonplussed I couldn't help laughing. After a second, he joined in.

"I suppose I shouldn't do that when Dad's not around

to defend himself—but he already knows I think he acts pompously. He says it's part of his job. Which I'm supposed to be doing now."

I'd met Jed only moments earlier, but already I knew he could never carry off pomposity. He did seem serious, though, about doing his father's job. His eyes were scanning the room.

"Where do you study?" he asked.

I pointed to the pair of chairs where Lord Reston and I had sat only the day before. I was delighted that Jed sat down immediately without doing the elaborate cat-and-mouse dance all my other instructors followed: "Princess, may I help you to your seat?" (Deep bow.) "May it be your pleasure that your humble servant be seated as well?" (Deep bow again.) Madame Bisset had told me that if anyone failed to show me the proper respect of that ridiculous little routine ("ridiculous" being my term for it, not hers) I should feign a fainting spell and call for a guard to have the cretin removed. I had never bothered to ask how I could call for a guard while fainting. I hastened to my chair for fear that Jed might realize his error and attempt to correct it. In the past weeks, I'd been "Princess"-ed and "humble servant"-ed enough to last a lifetime.

Jed was busy taking a slender booklet out of his jacket.

"Can you read?" he asked.

"Of course," I said, blushing indignantly, though there was no "of course" about it. Even in the palace—maybe especially in the palace—plenty of women couldn't read. And since I was a commoner—if Jed knew what I really was—he couldn't assume I'd even seen an alphabet, let alone ever opened a book.

"My father taught me," I said. "He collected old books, and sometimes I would help him appraise them. . . ." I was overcome with a flash of memory: my father and I, our heads bent close over an old book dusty and brittle with age, yet richly gilded, full of beautiful script and words that sang. The candlelight around us ebbed and flowed, and I felt like we were sitting in an ever-changing dome of light, while all around us was darkness. It was not one particular moment that I remembered, but dozens, for we had often looked at books together in the evenings before the Step-Evils arrived.

"Does he only buy books, or also sell?" Jed asked. "There are a few rare volumes of philosophy I've been looking for."

In truth, my father had had to sell almost as much as he bought. That was how he supported us. But, of course, I couldn't say that if I was supposed to be a princess.

"My father is dead," I blurted instead. The words brought back the pain I'd felt when I heard the news three years ago. I could still see Lucille clutching the letter and practically cackling, "The fool was trying to cross the Sualan border. For books!" And she'd rolled her eyes. Now I closed mine momentarily.

"I'm sorry," Jed said with an air of deep sincerity.

"Thank you," I said. I had not known what to do with condolences when the news was fresh, and I did not know now. I bent forward to look at the book in Jed's hand. It was the first one I had seen since coming to the castle, so I felt genuine eagerness. "What would you have me read?"

He showed me the title: *The Book of Faith.*

"My father has not showed you this?" he asked in puzzlement.

I shook my head.

"But he was instructing you in the official religion. He was to certify that you were a fit companion for the prince and would raise your offspring in the faith."

I started laughing as I hadn't since coming to the castle. I probably hadn't even laughed like that since before the Step-Evils entered my life.

"Religion?" I asked incredulously. "I thought he was teaching me royal genealogy. All those dull, dead kings—"

I was laughing so hard, even Jed had to smile.

"Aye, to my father 'tis much the same thing," he admitted.

My laughter turned into snorts, very nonroyal. I calmed myself.

"About the faith—," Jed began.

I began giggling again and calmed myself only to start again. And again. I was a fountain of hilarity, shooting out bursts of laughter every time Jed tried to speak. At last he gave up and laughed too.

6

After that, my days fell into a happier pattern. I still struggled to stay awake during needlepoint lessons, and Madame Bisset still corrected my pronunciation and my posture and my manners about fifty thousand times for every five minutes I spent with her. I still longed to go outside. (Madame Bisset turned down my timid request for riding lessons with a horrified sniff and the words: "A princess would never be without her carriage." Then she fainted.) And I still wished that Prince Charming and I could talk, even just once, without a chaperon there making us all stiff and formal and tongue-tied. But at least now, with Jed, I knew I had one person I could talk to in the castle.

As the days passed, I decided that the servant girl, Mary, was another. She began springing up at odd moments with odd bits of information about Lord Reston ("Criminy! Would you believe he heaved his pillow at the wall yesterday? And him a lord and all?") or touchingly eager offers of help. ("You don't need anything, do you?

Because if you did, I could get it for you. I've dusted the whole castle since breakfast, seems like, and now me mum says I'm allowed to do whatever I want.") I found myself telling her things I probably shouldn't have, because she was so much like a puppy dog bouncing around me, ready to fetch anything I wished without so much as a pat on the head for a reward.

"Vinegar will get that out," I told her one day when she informed me she wouldn't be around for a day or so because she'd been given dozens of stained napkins to wash.

"Yes, that's what me mum said," Mary answered. She squinted, an expression that made her features look even more unmatched than ever. "But how do you know? Is it true, what people say about you?"

"What people? What do they say?" I braced myself for Mary to accuse me of having washed plenty of dirty laundry in my lifetime, and of possessing no more royal blood than herself—an accusation that was certainly true. I was more than prepared to confess. But Mary was backing away from me in awe.

"Oh . . . nothing. Is . . ." She started timidly, then grinned with a bit more of her usual flippancy. "Is magic easier than vinegar?"

It was my turn to squint, puzzled. But Mary just melted away because yet another instructor was being shown into the room to teach me something I didn't want to know.

"Do you believe in magic?" I asked Jed later that morning when he showed up for my religion lesson.

"It depends," he said slowly. I was discovering that Jed never gave easy, automatic, or quick answers, but had to ponder out every side of things. "I believe there can be extraordinary events that ordinary humans tend to label as magic because we can't fully understand."

"And are you an ordinary human?" I teased.

He hesitated and seemed about to ask me something, then appeared to think better of it.

"I'm certainly no prince," he said. "Now, about that cat-echism I gave you . . ."

I recited it word for word, the list of twenty beliefs I was supposed to swear to that would make me a fit wife for the prince and a fit mother for a future king. This cate-chism was much longer, more formal, and less under-standable than the one children learned back in the village. Of course, that one ran: "I believe in God. He is good. I will obey Him"—so there was lots of room for improvisation. But I had a hard time believing that my ladies-in-waiting—the moronic Simprianna? the breath-takingly beautiful but addled Cyronna?—had spent much of their lives pondering "the transubstantiation of the Spirit" or "the resurrection of the physical being of our entities." For that matter, the king, queen, and Prince Charming didn't seem like the types to sit around consid-ering weighty religious matters, and they supposedly were in charge of the entire church.

"Good, ah, good." Jed nodded encouragingly. "That's really all you need."

I stared.

"So, that's it? I've—graduated?"

He looked away.

"No, no, of course not. Now that you know the creed, we have to make sure you understand it."

I breathed a sigh of relief. That could last at least until my wedding, if not until my dying day. Jed opened the *Book of Faith* between us and pointed at the first line of the catechism I had just recited. He opened his mouth to begin an explanation.

"I wasn't raised to be religious," I said suddenly.

"No?" Jed asked, typically patient with the interruption.

"No. My father was a doubter—he carried that around like a belief."

"So you're just reciting this? It means nothing to you?"

"No, no . . . I don't know. I knew people back in the village—I mean, where I come from—who had a great deal of faith, and it truly meant something. It made a difference." I told Jed about my neighbor Mrs. Branson of the ten children. Once, years ago, her husband broke his leg and couldn't work for many weeks, and they ran out of food. This was during a hard winter, and even if the Bransons hadn't been too proud to beg, there were few people who could spare enough for twelve extra people. So she prayed. And then that very night, food appeared on her doorstep. Several loaves of bread, a wheel of cheese, a cured ham. Enough to tide them over.

"Did she ever find out who left it?" Jed asked.

"No. But I knew. Those exact foods disappeared from

our larder. And my father's shoes were muddy in the morning, even though I'd cleaned them—I mean, they'd been cleaned—the night before."

Jed digested this story, which I'd never told anyone before. Lucille would have killed my father, had she known.

"I think you lost me," Jed said. "How does that story argue for belief? Maybe your neighbor should have just prayed to your father."

"Wouldn't have worked," I said. "He hated beggars. But her faith gave Mrs. Branson the sense of peace and dignity that even my father, a doubter, had to respect."

Jed nodded thoughtfully.

"I wasn't really raised to be religious either," he murmured after a moment.

I turned to him in astonishment.

"What? But your father is priest to the king!" I'd only recently learned that from Mary. So *that* was why he was supposed to be addressed as "His Excellency." I continued in my amazement, "After the king, he's the most powerful person in the church!"

Jed shrugged.

"State religion—you'll learn this—it's got nothing to do with God. It's all show. Smoke and mirrors. If any of these people really believed what they mumbled about, they'd go *do* something, instead of just talking."

"So what does that mean about you?" I teased. "Why aren't you doing something, instead of just talking?"

I thought we'd been friends long enough that I could

joke like that. But Jed flushed a deep red and turned shy, as if I'd just accused him of being sweet on some maiden.

"Well . . . uh . . . actually," he said, stumbling over his words, "there is something I'm . . . um . . . trying to find a way to do."

"What?" I asked, full of curiosity. I had no idea what he might say.

Jed looked down.

"You know about the Sualan War?" he asked softly.

If he hadn't been acting so strangely, I might have joked, "Do you take me for an imbecile?" Even the village idiot knew to curse Suala, because they were trying to take lands that belonged to our kingdom. At least, that's what everybody said. I sometimes wondered what Suala's version was. My father had once said—in the privacy of our own home—that the two kingdoms had been fighting for so long that they'd rendered the land useless to anyone.

"You want to fight in the war?" I asked incredulously. There were some who did—I remembered boys in my village who spoke of nothing but the glory they would earn in battle. But Jed didn't seem the type.

"No," he said, as if surprised I might suggest such a thing. "I wouldn't give a minute of my life for that. It's the refugees, the people who have been thrown off their lands by the war. Every time the battle lines shift, the people on the border lose crops, houses, barns—sometimes everything. And some of them have nowhere to go. So, I want to set up camps to take care of them, to make sure no one starves or freezes or dies because of what our kingdom is doing."

His eyes flashed, and I thought, *This is the key to Jed. This is the most important thing in the world to him.* The whole time I'd known him, which was about three weeks now, he'd seemed mopey and directionless, like an old sheepdog who'd been taken away from his herd. As nice as he'd been to me, I knew he didn't want to spend his life teaching pompous words to pretend princesses. So this was what he really wanted to do instead.

"Have you told anyone?" I asked. "Have you asked your father or the king or whoever—"

"Of course!" Jed said, so forcefully I jerked back against my brocaded chair.

"And?"

He shook his head mournfully.

"They put me off," he said. "They say they'll study the possibility; they'll draw up a committee to see what ought to be done; they'll think it over. . . . Not that they'd ever let *me* go, anyhow, because I'm supposed to be studying to take over my father's job. But meanwhile, people are dying."

I tilted my head to the side, considering.

"Why do you need anyone's permission? Why don't you just do it yourself?"

Jed gave me a condescending look, the first time *he'd* made me feel like the empty-headed piece of fluff everyone else seemed to expect me to be.

"I have no great wealth of my own," he said bitterly. "I

don't want to feed these people just for a day. I want to give them their lives back. But maybe you—"

Something crept into his voice, a slyness I did not associate with Jed.

"What?" I asked, my heart beating unusually fast.

"When you are queen—or maybe sooner than that, once you have the prince's confidence—maybe you can plead my cause for me. You could convince the prince to bankroll my refugee camps. It wouldn't take much, not compared with the vastness of the royal treasury. Not compared with what they're already spending on the war." Jed leaned forward, beseechingly. "Will you help?"

I felt a strange disappointment. What had I expected him to say? Given who I was, where I was, what I was—a female, now a female of the nobility—how else could I be expected to help? And I was no stranger to the power of pillow talk. Early on in my father's marriage to Lucille, while I still thought of the tangled relations in our household as a war that I could win, I had many times thought I'd convinced my father of something—that Corimunde and Griselda should be required to wash dishes with me, say—only to hear the decision reversed the next morning. I would watch my father and Lucille retire to his room together and imagine Lucille purring her arguments—"Oh, yes, I'm all for fairness, but Corimunde and Griselda have such delicate skin, an affliction Ella is fortunate not to suffer"—without me there to counter her. So now I was supposed to possess that—not real power, not the right to make any decisions myself, but the power of persuasion, when coupled with a kiss and a breathy whisper and the rest of what men and women do in bed? Unaccountably, the thought disgusted me.

It was a long moment before I realized Jed was still waiting for my answer. He was leaning so far forward in his chair that a small breath might knock him off and send him tumbling gracelessly to the floor. His expression was so full of hope, I wanted to cry.

"I'll—" I cleared my throat. "I'll do what I can."

7

That afternoon, while sitting with my ladies-in-waiting working on a particularly vexatious tapestry pattern, I couldn't get my conversation with Jed out of my mind. I jabbed my needle in and out, the loops of white thread accumulating as slowly as milk in a pail from an old cow. We were working on a scene of knights at a tournament, and my meager needlework skills had been exiled to the clouds in the sky. Simprianna, for all her mental deficiencies, was surprisingly brilliant at knowing where to stitch to make an expression look jubilant or defeated, so she was doing faces. I stopped for a second and watched her needle flying in and out, creating a sense of fervor on every visage.

Jed had looked just as fervent declaring his hopes for the refugee camps. I remembered thinking years ago, about the time my father married Lucille, that everyone must have something that matters to them more than anything else, that blinds them to everything else. How else to explain my father and Lucille? He was learned and honorable and true; she was base and lazy and greedy and mendacious. She was probably intelligent enough, but she did not care about knowledge, only gossip and fashion and getting her own way.

For a while I feared that what people whispered was true, that my father was lovesick, blinded to her faults by his desire to touch her skin, caress her body, join his to hers. (She was not bad-looking, if you didn't know her.) I don't think most twelve-year-olds want to think about their parents having intimate relations; how much worse that my father's relations were with Lucille. But then, by listening at doors and watching them together, I hit upon what I was sure was the truth.

Somehow she'd figured out that his books mattered most to him, and she'd been crafty enough to pretend to love them too. I believe she'd even promised to catalogue them for him—a task he'd been vowing to undertake for as long as I could remember but despaired of ever accomplishing. Of course, after they were married, her true views came out. I never saw anyone look as hurt as he did the day she shoved away a particularly rare book he was showing her and snarled, "Get that vile, dusty thing away from me."

I'm ashamed to say I tried to deepen the hurt, reporting to him every inane, vicious, and ignorant comment she had ever made about him or his books. Childishly, I thought he could just undo his mistake, unmarry her. I didn't understand honor and promises—or didn't want to. He began traveling a lot more, to search for ever-rarer books, but also to avoid Lucille. And that was what he was doing when he died.

So that was my father's passion and where it led him. And now I knew Jed's. Wanting to help those hurt by the war was a noble cause, to be sure. Why did that bother me? Was it because I didn't have a cause of my own? Was I supposed to?

I brought my needle in and out dozens of times, pondering that question. I am engaged, I reminded myself. Prince Charming is supposed to be your passion. No—he *is* your passion. You love him.

Somehow, though, it seemed like I needed more. Maybe it was because I'd won him too easily. I'd known girls in my village who'd set their hearts on a particular boy, then plotted their days so they'd be coming out of the baker's just in time to bump into their beloved as he was leaving the miller's. They'd save and scrimp for weeks to have enough sugar to bake a pie for their intended, only to say, giggling, "Oh, it was just some extra we had—thought you might want it," when the pie was delivered, as if any sign of wanting him would scare him off (which it sometimes did).

I had hardly plotted to ensnare the prince. I'd never even dreamed it was possible. I'd just gone to the ball as a lark, partly out of curiosity, partly to spite Lucille. (Would I have cared about going if she hadn't forbidden me?)

I felt a surge of triumph—oh, how I had spited her. Then I was instantly ashamed. Perhaps, truly, what mattered most to me was beating Lucille. It didn't seem like a very worthy cause. As much as she'd messed up the last five years of my life, Lucille had problems of her own. Now that I was in the castle, and she was still in the village, I shouldn't think of her as the enemy anymore. I should probably just pity her and find some other goal to focus on. But what?

My thread tangled then, and I had to interrupt a discussion about dressing gowns to get Simprianna to help me unsnarl it. (She was also quite skilled at that. I suppose I was too hard on her, considering her an absolute simpleton.) I apologized profusely to Simprianna, as if that could make up for all the cruel things I'd ever thought about Lucille.

"I'm so sorry. I don't know how it happened."

Silently Simprianna picked at the knots in my thread with a perfectly curved fingernail. Then she began to pull out my last row of stitches.

"Wait," I said. "Why—" Then I saw a snarl that I hadn't even noticed at the beginning of the row. All my stitches since had been useless.

"Oh," I said. "I see. I'm sorry about that too. I guess my mind was wandering."

Simprianna barely glanced up.

"Aye, Princess," she sighed. "Can you not ask your fairy godmother for help?"

"My what?" I asked.

She and a few of the others giggled. I heard someone whisper, on the other side of the tapestry, "Well, of course she has to pretend she doesn't know. . . ."

"Nothing, Princess," Simprianna murmured, keeping her eyes on her work.

I looked around. All twelve of the other ladies had their heads bent low over the tapestry. Nobody was going to enlighten me. But—fairy godmother? It reminded me of Mary asking about magic. I decided the castle folk, servants and nobility alike, were a superstitious lot. I wish I had had a fairy godmother to protect me all those years I lived with the Step-Evils. Of course, I wouldn't need one now.

Would I?

8

Once he'd shared his dream for the refugee
camps, Jed seemed to feel he could tell me anything. My daily religion lessons were taken up
less and less with talk of the trinity or the "cor-
poreal evidence of His Holiness"—whatever that
meant—and more and more with banter, jokes,
and Jed's tales about his childhood.

"I feel sorry for any child who didn't get to
grow up in this castle," he said one sunny morning a few weeks after he'd taken over for his
father.

"Why?" I asked in surprise. By then, Jed
surely realized my own childhood had taken
place outside of any palace walls. And if he
didn't, I hardly cared if he found out. "I would
think a child in this castle was to be pitied. All
those people around telling you to sit up straight,
don't speak while the minister of the treasury
is speaking, and don't spill your soup on the
foreign ambassador or it'll start a war—"

Jed laughed.

"Yes, there was rather too much of that for

my taste. But we children were kept mostly out of sight, so we didn't have to worry about foreign policy. What I meant was . . . have you never noticed the length of the banisters on the main staircase?"

I nodded, remembering my awe the night of the ball at the sight of the grand staircase, which rose from the entrance hall to a spot that would be three stories higher in a normal house. The tallest man I'd ever seen, a carpenter in my village called Tom the Giant, could have lain down on a step with neither his head nor his feet touching the sides. And the staircase was lined on each side by pillars and a banister of rare polished wood that I knew from Lord Reston's lectures had been brought from faraway lands decades ago.

"You used to slide down the banisters," I gasped. I did not confess that I had longed to do that very thing from the moment I'd seen them. But I'd never been near the banisters when there weren't at least a dozen others with me. And while it would be delightful to see the scandalized expression on Madame Bisset's face, I did still want to marry the prince. Not to mention, to continue living. Considering that I'd been confined to my room for letting my petticoat slip out and show beneath my skirt for an instant, I had a feeling Madame Bisset would view banister sliding by a princess as a crime worthy of execution.

"Was it as much fun as it looks?" I asked Jed.

He grinned in a way that made me think he must have been an awfully ornery little boy.

"Oh, yes. My brothers and I would sneak out at night and have races, one of us on each side."

"Brothers?" I asked.

"I have three. All younger, and all away at school in the East," he said.

"So, will they all become priests like you?" I teased.

He grimaced.

"No, 'tis only the oldest who must follow his father's career. They may do as they wish. *They* would be allowed to work with the war refugees, as I may not. If any of them wanted to. Which they don't."

"What do they want?" I asked.

He laughed.

"To be priest to the king. The one thing they won't be allowed. What's that your friend, the servant girl, is always saying?"

I'd told him about Mary.

"Oh, you mean"—I mustered up my best imitation of her voice—"don't that beat all?"

We laughed together, at either my poor imitation of Mary's words or the perversity of Jed's brothers.

"I wish—," I started, and immediately clamped my mouth shut. For what I had intended to say was, "I wish I could laugh this way with the prince. I wish I felt as close to him as I do to you." I didn't need Madame Bisset around to tell me those were inappropriate words, indecent thoughts. But I shouldn't worry. The prince and I would feel close as soon as we could be together without a chaperon. I was just lucky that Jed, being a priest in training, didn't need to be chaperoned in my presence as well.

"What do you wish, milady?" Jed asked with mock formality.

Because I had to say something, I blurted out, "I wish I knew if you know the truth about me."

I saw a gleam of interest in his eyes, as if he'd been longing to discuss this but hadn't felt he could bring it up himself. In that instant, I decided to tell him everything.

"Well, I do know," he started slowly and carefully, peering straight into my eyes, "that you're not a Domulian princess, as is claimed."

"And how do you know that?" I asked.

He began ticking off the reasons on his fingers.

"One, Domulia is the farthest land we know of, and you probably could not have had time to hear of the ball and travel here between the time it was announced and the time it was held."

"Maybe I have magical powers," I teased.

He seemed strangely jolted by that, but went on.

"Two, Domulian princesses are famously ugly and wart covered and you, well, are not. Either one. Ugly or wart covered."

It was the first time he'd mentioned my appearance since the day we met. His glance made me uncomfortable.

"And?" I prompted.

"Three, you once told me a story about your father giving food away to a hungry neighbor. Kings do not live near hungry people, and if they do, they don't feed them. They employ them. Or banish them."

"But maybe my father was an extraordinary king," I argued.

Jed ignored that.

"And, four, you do not remember this, because I was far in the background, practically out of sight, but I was there the day the prince put the slipper on your foot and whisked you away to the palace."

I blushed. How had I missed him? Of course, that day I'd had eyes only for the prince. I vaguely recalled that he'd had a crowd of retainers with him, but they had seemed more like props than people.

"You were? Why?"

"One of my royal duties," Jed said with a shrug. "I was supposed to be getting experience advising the prince. Of course, all my advice was disregarded. I said that since your entire village knew about you, the king should announce to the world that his son was marrying a commoner, in a show of unity with his people or some such thing. I thought it would be good for the royal image in the kingdom. But it was decided that acknowledging the truth would insult all the kings who'd hoped to marry off their daughters to Charming. As it is, I'm sure all the foreign kings have heard the rumors and are insulted, but they can't confront the Charmings without calling them liars."

For just that instant, I could imagine Jed as a royal adviser. He would give well-reasoned counsel, but he wouldn't care enough to be persuasive. Because he'd always be thinking about the refugee camps instead.

"Why—" I gulped, not quite sure I had the nerve to voice my question. But this might be my only opportunity. "Why *is* the prince willing to marry a mere commoner?"

I wanted Jed to look me in the eye and say, "Because he's fallen head over heels in love with you. Don't you know? Everybody's talking about it. Men older than my grandfather say they've never seen a prince so deeply in love."

But Jed wouldn't meet my gaze.

"I'd guess it's because you're not ugly and wart covered like a Domulian princess," he mumbled, staring fixedly at the fire.

There was a silence between us, and I felt as tongue-tied and uncomfortable as I often did with the prince. Then Jed looked up and gave me a solid grin.

"So. Do you have magical powers or was there a fairy godmother helping you at the ball, the way everyone claims?" he asked.

9

"What?" I asked, flabbergasted. It had been one thing to hear Mary and Simprianna talk about magic and fairy godmothers as if such things truly existed. They were uneducated, bound to be superstitious. Simprianna also couldn't count beyond ten. But Jed was learned. He was practical. He was a man.

"You've not heard the story going around the palace?" he asked. "About how you got to come to the ball when your evil stepmother had locked you in the cellar?"

"Lucille isn't e—," I started to protest, in an unusual surge of loyalty. Then I remembered Jed must have seen her, in all her frilly purple dressing-gown glory, the day I left. So he knew. "Well, she didn't lock me in the cellar. She just told me I had to scrub it out by hand before she and Griselda and Corimunde returned."

"All right," Jed said. "Close enough. And you were in tears about it. But then your fairy godmother appeared."

I gave him a "You have got to be kidding" look, but let him keep talking.

"Your fairy godmother appeared and waved her magic wand and turned your rags into a ball gown, complete with glass slippers. Then she took a pumpkin and some mice and turned them into a carriage and horses. But she said her magic could last only until midnight—that's why you were in such a rush to leave at the stroke of twelve that you left one of your glass slippers behind. Which, everyone knows, is how the prince found you."

By the time Jed got to the one detail that was true, I was laughing so hard tears were streaming down my face.

"Some . . . someone . . . actually . . . believes that?" I finally sputtered between giggles.

"It's more plausible than you as a Domulian princess," Jed said with a grin. "What's the truth?"

"Well," I started slowly, "it wasn't quite that exciting."

And yet, I felt a surge of exhilaration just thinking about that night. Not just because I'd met the prince and fallen in love and started on my course toward happiness ever after, but because I'd made something happen. I'd done something everybody had told me I couldn't. I'd changed my life all by myself. Having a fairy godmother would have ruined everything.

"Promise you won't tell anyone?" I said. "I mean, it probably doesn't matter to anyone else, but if the king and queen and the prince still want to keep up the fiction that I'm foreign royalty, I don't want to spread my story."

Jed nodded. "Of course," he said.

I started my tale.

"Once upon a time," I said mischievously, wrinkling my nose so Jed would know I was making fun of the whole thing, "I was just a poor girl in rags. . . ."

But somehow remembering everything transported me back, and I quickly settled into seriousness. I wasn't even pretending to be Princess Cynthiana Eleanora anymore. I was myself again, Ella Brown, always hungry, always cold, always angry at my stepmother's and stepsisters' cruelties. . . .

10

I was scrubbing the kitchen floor when the invitation arrived by royal herald. There was a smart rap at the front door, and I began debating which would make Lucille angrier: me answering the door with a kerchief around my head and water dripping from the bottom of my skirt, or me not answering the door at all and leaving her or Corimunde or Griselda to the indignity of opening it themselves. I hadn't decided yet when I heard Corimunde gasp.

"Look, Gris, out the window."

I heard a flurry of swishing skirts and petticoats from the sitting room as they both apparently raced to the door. Thanks to a steady diet of bonbons, they each weighed twice what I did, and they rarely bestirred themselves for anything except to waddle into the dining room for their next meal. So I was sure whatever Corimunde was gasping about was worth a peek. Opening the kitchen door a crack, I had a direct view of the young, flaxen-haired man on the doorstep. He was stunningly handsome, with a physique I'd seen only in my father's books about ancient gods and heroes. He wore tight black pants and a rich scarlet tailcoat, with a fancy design in gold on every pocket and lapel. He held a trumpet to his lips and blew two short blasts, then one long note of exquisite tone.

"Your . . . Your Highness." Corimunde was flustered, even for her.

"S-s-sir," Griselda stuttered.

The man gave them both looks of withering scorn.

"Hear ye, hear ye," he boomed in a deep voice that somehow conveyed that he didn't feel Corimunde and Griselda were worthy of his message, but that he was not one to shirk his work and would speak as grandly to them as he did to anyone else. "The king and queen hereby invite every young maiden in the kingdom to a ball in honor of their son, Prince Charming, on Saturday night four weeks hence, beginning at eight o'clock in the evening."

"Four weeks hence—would that be the twenty-second?" Griselda ventured timidly.

"No, silly, the twenty-third," corrected Corimunde. "The Saturday would have to be the twenty-third, because today's the . . . uh . . . let's see, I think it's the—"

"Four weeks hence," the herald repeated firmly and bowed low, preparing to go.

"Excuse me," I said from my post in the kitchen. "Did you say *every* young maiden?"

The herald looked up. By his face, I could tell he was preparing to give a disgusted retort, perhaps questioning the hearing of all the women in our household. But when he saw me, his expression softened into something I didn't want to acknowledge as pity.

"Aye, miss," he said in an almost gentle tone. "Every young maiden."

"Now, wait just a minute." It was Lucille, sweeping down from upstairs, where she'd been resting with a sick headache. "I would never dream of contradicting someone of your"—she looked him up and down, almost lecher-ously—"your *stature,* but surely you don't mean that the king and queen would want their ball cluttered with mere beggars and servants and ragamuffins. My heavens—such squalor. Surely they mean only young ladies of high social standing and good breeding. Like my lovely daughters." She waved her hand gracefully toward Griselda and Corimunde who, to their credit, at least attempted to stand up straight. Corimunde even stopped picking her nose momentarily.

The royal herald looked from Lucille to my stepsisters to me.

"The king has invited *every* young maiden," he said. "You wish perhaps to contradict the king?"

"Well, no, but—" Lucille laughed gently, trying to make him look foolish. "Perhaps you misunderstood."

"I did not," the herald said adamantly. "Now, if you will excuse me. Good day."

He swept low again and departed. Corimunde and Griselda fell immediately to squabbling. "Now, why did you say that about the twenty-third? You could have looked it up on a calendar when he was gone—"

"Oh, but I wanted to be sure—"

"Silence!" Lucille barked.

Corimunde and Griselda both shut up and peered up at her, still standing imperially on the stairs. Lucille's command had certainly sounded strong enough, but now she began swaying weakly.

"Oh, help me sit down, girls," she demanded. Her daughters sprang to her side as quickly as they could, given their bulk. "Oh, there is so much to do, it's a shame I'm so indisposed. . . . Let me think. . . ."

She held the back of her hand dramatically against her brow. Then she seemed to receive an invisible surge of strength and screeched, "Ella! Ella! Oh, where is that wretched creature?"

Since I was by then standing at the bottom of the stairs, in plain sight, her performance was hardly necessary.

"Ye-es?" I said, stretching the word out to sound as insolent as possible.

"Say 'Yes, Madame' when addressing your betters," she snapped. "How many times do I have to tell you that?"

"You are older than me. You have more power than me. But you are *not* my better," I snapped back. "How many times do I have to tell *you* that?"

She narrowed her eyes, obviously contemplating punishments. Being sent to bed without supper, her usual choice, had already been doled out for the day, because I had not folded the sheets with the military precision she expected. She should have known better than to use up the biggest gun in her arsenal before nine o'clock in the morning.

"No lunch for you today," she said. I did not care. Lunch was soup and bread, which I would prepare and serve. How would she know if I ate some in the kitchen?

But Lucille seemed pleased with herself. Her voice softened.

"Be a dear and bring me a cool cloth for my forehead," she said. Then, with a sweet smile, she added, "And don't even think about going to that ball."

"Oh, so you think you can control my thoughts now too?" I retorted.

"Fine. Think all you want," she said with a shrug. "But I can assure you, you won't go."

"I will!"

"Wearing what? That?" She laughed, tilting her head back with such abandon, I was sure her sick headache was faked. After a long pause, proving just how slow they were on the uptake, Corimunde and Griselda joined in.

"Can you see *her* at a royal ball?" Corimunde twittered.

"In those rags?" Griselda replied unoriginally.

They sounded like a pair of dimwitted birds. But they had a point. I was wearing my only dress. It had once been nice, back when my father was alive. But after I'd spent two years in it carrying wood in, carrying ashes out, scouring pots, scrubbing floors, boiling laundry, and doing everything else that needed to be done since Lucille had dismissed all our servants as "an unnecessary expense," even I could no longer discern the pattern in the dress's threadbare weave. Even I was at pains to see how it could possibly be mended again, just to keep me decent. I had kept silent about it, making it a battle of wills: Would Lucille buy me something new before I was forced to go about in my underclothes? Maybe the ball would force her hand.

"You'll buy ball gowns for Corimunde and Griselda," I said. "So you shall buy one for me as well."

Lucille's laughter swelled again.

"Why?" she said. "So I can be held responsible for forcing a beggar upon the prince? Never!"

I turned on my heel, the laughter seeming to follow me down the hall. I did not get Lucille's cool cloth—I wagered she'd forgotten it as well. But I was muttering, "I will go. I'll show you. You'll see."

So my plot began.

In the attic, I knew, my mother's wedding gown had lain untouched for years. The memories it evoked had been too painful for my father, too sacred for me. I don't think any of the Step-Evils even knew it was there. (Had any of them ever stepped foot in the attic, with all its dust and spiders?) Late that night, after I knew they were all asleep, I crept up the stairs, pulled the gown out of the trunk, and tried it on. I had only moonlight to see by, and no mirror, but I could feel the elegance of the folds of satin against my skin. I felt like a different person—not Ella Brown, former tomboy and bookworm and current all-purpose drudge, not Cinders-Ella, as Corimunde and Griselda sometimes derisively called me—but an Eleanora, maybe even a Princess Eleanora. Had my mother felt this elegant, walking down the aisle with my father? I tried to imagine it, taking halting, silent steps around the attic. But the sight of my dirty bare feet poking out from beneath the skirt ruined the effect. If I went to the ball, what would I do about shoes?

I bent over the trunk to search for whatever footwear my mother had worn, and the dress slipped forward. I could feel it gaping open at the bodice. I looked down and could see clear to my thin, bare thighs. Of course. The dress was much too big on me. My mother had been well nourished and healthy, and I had been living for the past two years on whatever food I could pilfer from the kitchen without Lucille noticing. When was the last time I *hadn't* been ordered to bed without supper?

I resolved then and there that the ball was just a first step. Two years was more than enough time to serve as a slave in my own home. I had been holding on to my father's memories and my father's house, doing the work Lucille ordered me to do with enough insolence and back talk that I was sure she'd have to break down and admit I had rights of my own. But staring down at my emaciated rib cage, I realized suddenly that Lucille was winning. No—Lucille had won. She had reduced me—literally reduced me—to feeling that I didn't deserve food or a new ball gown or a life.

Dizzily I sat down and reviewed my choices. I could walk away. I could hire myself out as a servant—I certainly had enough experience. But I didn't want to spend the rest of my life hauling ashes. I could get married—the butcher's boy was a willing candidate, if not a particularly desirable one. But I'd seen enough of loveless marriage to know that that wasn't what I wanted. No, I'd wait for someone capable of making me swoon. That left only one possibility, and a slim one at that: Could I find work as a tutor of sorts for rich children? If I brushed up on my Latin and Greek, I was sure I could do that quite well. I could save my money and someday come back and buy the house from Lucille. That way, leaving wouldn't be like giving up. The only problem was, I didn't know anyone willing to pay to have their children educated.

Maybe I could meet someone at the ball.

That decided, I felt much better and resumed digging through the trunk.

11

Over the next two weeks, I planned my strategy with more forethought than some kings put into entire wars. I took in my mother's dress, sewing late at night by the light of a precious candle. I considered reshaping it somehow, to match the current beruffled, bespangled fashions I saw in the books Griselda and Corimunde had begun poring over endlessly. But I had so little faith in my dressmaking skills, and such great fear of ruining one of the few things I had of my mother's, that I dared not cut into the fabric at all. So I was sure my upper body would look like a stick with breasts above the great tulip flower of the skirt. My waist had shrunk to such a degree that I could practically circle it with my own hands. But that could not be helped.

I'd also found long, elegant gloves in my mother's trunk—a stroke of good fortune, since my hands were rough and chapped and cracked from the constant work. With gloves, no one would ever know. Not that it mattered, unless I did find a potential employer at the ball.

For a long time I was stymied on the matter of shoes, since my mother's wedding slippers flapped on my small feet like sailboats. My sole footwear was a pair of old boots of my father's, which I laced high up on my legs just to keep them on. They would hardly do. I had practically decided to go barefoot, and just keep my feet out of sight, when I happened to pass the glassblower's shop one day on my way to the market. Jonas, the village glassblower, was a pompous fellow, and that day he was out in the street bragging of the quality of his work.

"I can make anything," he boasted to his neighbor, the cartwright. "Name an item, any item, and I wager I can make it."

"Glass slippers I can walk in without breaking them," I said, slipping between them.

The cartwright, Harold, looked from Jonas to me.

"Aye," Harold said. "I'd put some money on that."

Jonas looked startled, and I saw a flash of uncertainty cross his face. Then the greed took over.

"How much?" he asked.

Harold and Jonas began haggling. I could tell each was confident. They pushed the wager to ten pounds.

"How long will it take?" I asked. Lucille had been watching me more closely than ever now. I think she suspected something. If I took a minute more than my allotted hour for marketing, she'd be screaming at me as soon as I walked in the door.

"Half an hour," Jonas said. "Then another fifteen minutes for them to fully cool."

"I'll be back, then," I said, though I longed to stay and watch. Glassblowing had always fascinated me. What if Jonas needed an apprentice? All the way to the market, I toyed with the idea of asking him. But, as much fun as the work might be, I didn't relish the notion of working with someone as arrogant as him. And I'd never heard of any of the craftsmen in the village apprenticing girls. Just boys. No, I'd stick with the tutoring plan. After the ball.

I rushed through the shopping, taking even less care than usual sorting through the turnips and rutabagas. It was spring, and fresh greens were available out in the meadows, so the shopkeepers were trying to get rid of last autumn's leftovers at practically any price. But I didn't want to think about feeding the Step-Evils when there were glass slippers to be had. I stuffed vegetables into my sack without looking at them.

"Ah, the girl who will win me ten pounds," Jonas proclaimed as I returned to his shop. He presented the slippers to me on a velvet pillow. They were stunning, catching the sunlight from every angle. To my untrained eyes, they looked like diamonds. Jonas leaned his head close to mine. "Just don't come down too hard on the heels."

"I won't," I promised. I bit my lip, then said the words I'd been rehearsing since I left the market. "But if I win the money for you, I get to keep the glass slippers."

Jonas squinted, sizing me up. I tried to look resolute. I must have succeeded, because Jonas slowly nodded.

"Aye," he said. "If you win."

I turned around, and it seemed that every man, woman, or child within three blocks was lined up outside the glassblower's door.

"Six steps," Jonas said. "That's what Harold and me agreed on."

I took a deep breath and slipped the shoes on. They were not comfortable. But they held together as I stepped out the door.

"One!" the crowd shouted. "Two!"

I kept my eyes on my feet, trying to avoid getting the heels caught between cobblestones.

"Three! Four!"

For the first time, I considered what would happen if the shoes broke. Would I be digging shards of glass out of my feet the rest of my life?

"Five!"

I stepped gingerly, my ankles wobbling.

"Six!"

The crowd burst into cheers, and Jonas let out a triumphant whoop. For the first time I looked up. Those who weren't cheering were giving me strange looks, and I realized what a sight I must be, in rags and glass slippers. I stepped out of the shoes and went to find Jonas, who was collecting money not just from Harold, but from a whole lineup of men.

"Thank you," I said.

"I'll take those now," he said, reaching for the shoes.

"But you said—," I protested.

"A misunderstanding," he said, his grip tightening on

the shoes. "What's a beggar like you need glass slippers for? I can sell these for good money."

I drew myself to my full height and glared.

"You think I misunderstood my deal with you?" I asked. "Perhaps all these people did too, then. You said I could keep the shoes if I won the bet for you. If I don't keep the shoes, you must not have won the bet."

I could remember my father attempting to teach me logic, years ago, and I didn't think my argument would hold up as a formal proof. But it worked against Jonas, because the crowd around him began to grumble. "What? We don't have to pay?" "You trying to cheat the girl, Jonas?" "You cheating us?"

Jonas let go of the shoes.

"Very well," he said tightly.

I turned and ran, before he changed his mind. It wasn't very dignified. But I had my shoes now.

The day of the ball came. Griselda and Corimunde spent the entire day preparing or, rather, demanding that I prepare them. I curled their limp, mousy locks at least six times apiece, trying to get the curls to hold. At six o'clock, I helped them into their dresses, which were so covered with ruffles and ribbons that they both looked like giant wedding cakes with heads on top. I stitched up the back of Corimunde's dress where she ripped out a seam getting into it. I fastened and then unfastened and then refastened the hook at the back of Griselda's neck when she complained, "It's too tight—it's too loose—it's too tight. . . ." I personally placed forkfuls of food in their mouths when they got hungry and Lucille admonished them not to eat for fear of mussing their dresses.

If I hadn't hated them before, I truly despised them now. I thought I could never be happier than I was at half past seven, when their hired carriage drove up and Lucille crowed, "Girls! Time to see and be seen!"—and they were off.

Lucille leaned her head back in the door and bellowed, "Remember! Scrub the entire cellar before we're back!"

I made a face she couldn't see. And as soon as she let the door close, I scurried up the stairs, scrubbed my face and hands and feet, and pulled my mother's dress over my head. I piled my hair atop my head and tied it with a thin blue ribbon Griselda would neither recognize nor miss. I laced my father's boots onto my feet, for it was a good half-hour walk to the castle, and I hardly planned to do that in glass slippers. I tucked the slippers under my arm and took off.

It was a pleasant evening, unseasonably warm. Birds were singing in the trees, and I remember feeling incredibly free. When was the last time I'd spent a half hour outdoors, all by myself, with no errands to run for Lucille? I thought of the cellar waiting to be scrubbed, and I grimaced. It was a long, dirty job, but surely if I left the ball by midnight, I could have it done before morning. If I was lucky, Lucille wouldn't check before then.

And if I wasn't lucky—what if Lucille or Corimunde or Griselda saw me at the ball? I tossed my head and decided I didn't care. I was leaving anyway. Somehow.

This night would mark my declaration of independence from Lucille. One way or another, I would not go back to being her slave.

When I was in sight of the castle, I took my father's boots off my now-blistered feet and pulled on the glass slippers. They were still anything but cozy. I reconsidered the barefoot notion, until I looked down and saw how lovely the slippers were, sparkling in the last gleams of twilight. At least they didn't rub the same places the boots had.

I hid the boots behind a tree and stood there for a moment, watching luxurious carriages pull up to the castle gates and discharge girls like me, most of them obviously unaccustomed to finery. They were all in giggly bunches: "Coo! Get a load of me in a ball gown!" "Aye, Jane, you're a fine sight. You gonna think you're too good to slop the hogs now?"

Some of them did, indeed, look ridiculous and out of place. But all of them at least had carriages. No one arrived on foot. I watched the carriages circle around the curved driveway and park, evidently planning to wait there until the ball ended and it was time to take all their passengers back home to their lives as serving girls and counter girls and scullery maids. Once they tied their horses up, the drivers began milling about alongside the driveway, talking and laughing at the spectacle of dozens of girls dressed to kill. I slipped over to the nearest driver, who was bent over one of his horse's shoes.

"Sir." I cleared my throat. "Sir, for a farthing, would

you take me to the castle gate in your carriage?"

He looked up, bug-eyed.

"Why, miss, I'd be honored to."

He helped me up into the carriage and snapped the reins smartly against his horses' backs. They jerked, as if surprised to be working again so soon. But they perked up and pranced over to the gate. The driver helped me out.

"Thank you so much. I'm sorry I can't afford any more."

He waved away my apologies.

"No matter. If you're out by midnight, I can drive you back a ways too. Someone like you needs to leave in elegance."

"But I don't have any more money."

"No matter," he said again. "My privilege."

I began climbing the castle stairs behind a gaggle of ruffly skirts. The doorman directed the girls in front of me to the left. He sent me to the right, and I wondered if that was a sign that I wasn't dressed well enough.

Then I caught sight of a vast wall of mirror in front of me. It reflected back a radiant, statuesque woman in an ivory dress much like mine. I honestly began looking around for the woman to ask if she was wearing her mother's wedding dress too. It took me a full minute to realize that woman was me. I hadn't looked in a mirror in a long time, and I had, well, grown. My cheeks were flushed from the walk and the excitement, and my hair, though slightly mussed, was still sleek and silken. The curls that had escaped from my ribbon looked as though they were supposed to be that way. The dress clung in all the right places, and as slender as I'd become, I was still plenty large where I needed to be.

I was beautiful. Truly beautiful.

I was still reeling from the shock of that notion when a fussy little man in a velvet waistcoat approached me.

"And how shall we announce you?" he asked.

"A-announce?" I stammered, as stupidly as Griselda or Corimunde.

"Your *name*," he said, as though he expected women to be stupid.

I watched an exquisitely dressed woman in front of me stand in an entryway while a deep voice called out, "Esmeralda Maria von Drappia."

She curtsied, and it sounded as though an entire village was applauding her. Then she glided into the ballroom.

So, I was to be announced too. The Step-Evils would know I was here. Well, so be it. My chin shot defiantly into the air.

"Just say Cinders-Ella is here," I said.

The man raised one eyebrow but nodded. He gave me a little push, and then I was standing in the entrance, blinded by the spotlights.

"Cinderella," the voice called out.

Numbly I moved forward, trying to get into the shadows so I could see. But almost instantly, a man took my hand.

"May I have this dance?"

I nodded, too stunned to speak. Evidently no words

were needed. The man took my other hand and whirled me along with the music.

I have not danced much, so at first it took all my concentration to follow his lead. But he had all the skill I lacked. Soon I could think and dance both, just by letting him take control. I examined my partner. He had a wide chest, a cleft chin, a strong jaw, brilliant blue eyes, golden hair, a gleaming crown. I gasped.

"You're the prince," I said.

"Yes," he said, and I liked the way he said it, very simply. He didn't boast. He didn't apologize the way I thought I would have if I'd been royalty: "Yes, but please don't let it make you think any differently of me." My heart beat fast. I hoped Lucille saw me dancing with the prince. But when I tried to look around to see if any of the Step-Evils were watching, I began to lose the time of the waltz, and nearly stumbled. I focused on the prince again. Because of my fragile glass slippers, I had to lean into him. I hoped he didn't think me forward.

The song ended with a whisper of violins, and I expected the prince to move on to another girl. But he peered deep into my eyes and murmured, "Again?"

I felt a thrill and murmured back, "Yes." Surely Lucille would see me now.

Somehow we ended up dancing every dance together. My feet were practically bloodied with the rubbing of the slippers, and I asked to sit down. The prince led me out onto a terrace, just him and me. From there I could see the moonlight and starshine and fields of roses. I looked back toward the castle and saw suddenly that there were two ballrooms facing the terrace. The first, where I'd been, was small and intimate. The other was large and packed. I caught sight of a fuchsia ruffle—yes, Griselda and Corimunde were in the other ballroom. So they hadn't seen me.

The prince began gently tracing the outline of my face with his finger, turning my face toward him.

"You're very beautiful," he whispered in a reverent tone.

I wanted to say, "You are too," but I knew that was wrong, because he was handsome, not beautiful. And then I couldn't say anything, because his hands had moved to the back of my head and were pulling me closer, and then suddenly he was kissing me, and I couldn't think of any words, only of him. Somehow he lifted me up, and we were dancing again, out on the terrace, under the stars. I could hear the music from the ballroom, light and beautiful. And then I heard something else, a rumbling *Dong, dong, dong* . . .

I pulled back and stared up at the palace clock.

"Oh, no. Is it midnight?" I asked.

The prince looked at me in a puzzled way.

"It is!" I said. "Oh, no. I'm so sorry. I have to leave. I have to leave by midnight. It's a silly thing, but still—I've had such fun with you. It's just as well—you probably need to dance with all the others. Good-bye—thank you—"

"You cannot leave," the prince said, attempting to pull me close again. I jerked away.

"Yes, I must. I'm sorry. So sorry—"

I flew through the door, back through the ballroom, and out the front door. I raced down the steps, forgetting to come down easy on the glass heels. I felt one shoe give, ever so slightly, and I shook it off so it wouldn't break. I didn't have time to pick it up, so I just left it there, on the castle steps. I saw the kind driver who'd helped me before, waiting at the gate.

"Do you have time?" I asked him. "Before your real customers come?"

He nodded and helped me in, and his horses practically galloped away.

He dropped me off at the tree where I'd left my boots. And I walked home and scrubbed the cellar as fast as I could. I heard the Step-Evils arrive home at three, grumbling that they'd barely seen the prince, and wasn't the food perfectly awful?

12

When I finished my story, I was surprised to look up and see Jed, instead of the dark, dirty walls of the cellar back home. I'd gotten so involved in the telling, I'd practically forgotten my story was all over, it had ended happily, I was in the castle for good now. I blinked several times, as blinded as someone walking into a dim hovel from bright sunshine. That's probably why I couldn't read the strange expression on Jed's face. Or maybe I was just confused. When I finally stopped blinking, he looked the same as ever—thoughtful, curious, and kind.

"And then?" he asked.

"You know the rest," I said. "You were there, I guess. The next afternoon, the prince came with my shoe and carried me off."

Jed leaned forward intently.

"But before that—did you tell Lucille you were leaving? Did you find someplace else to go?"

"I barely had a day," I said. "Not even that, because Lucille and the girls slept in, far past noon, and it was barely midafternoon when the prince showed up."

But his question made me defensive. I didn't want to admit to Jed that I'd spent that morning mooning over the prince, reliving every dance, every glance. I'd carried in wood dreaming of the kiss on the terrace; I'd carried out ashes remembering the feel of his hand on my back, guiding me across the dance floor. There was part of me that held back, pragmatically chiding myself, "What do you think you're doing? You'll never see the prince again, unless it's from a distance, when he's up on the castle balcony making a royal proclamation, and you're down in the crowd with all the other commoners. Someday you can tell your grandchildren about dancing with the prince. But for now, you've got other things to think about." And then I'd scraped my knuckles on the washboard, because I was distracted remembering the timbre of the prince's voice when he said, "May I have this dance?"

Jed cleared his throat, but his voice still came out half cracked.

"So that's how you got here," he said. He grinned, a gleam of mischief returning to his eye. "I can't say your story's that much less incredible than the ones about fairy godmothers and magic pumpkins."

"But it's the truth," I said. Impulsively, I reached for Jed's hand and squeezed it. "Don't you believe me? I know the truth has to be secret, but can't you get someone to stop all those rumors?"

Jed jerked back his hand, and I instantly felt ashamed, as though I'd done something improper.

"Princess," he said, with unusual emphasis. He never called me "Princess." "Nobody can stop those rumors. People would rather believe in fairy godmothers and . . . and . . . well, divine intervention, if you will—than to think that you took charge of your own destiny."

Later, after Jed had left, I lay down on my bed, stared up at the arc of canopy over my head, and thought about what he'd said. Had I taken charge of my own destiny? Sure, I'd found a way to go to the ball against Lucille's wishes. But the rest—the prince dancing with me, the prince bringing my shoe and seeking my hand in marriage—that had been far beyond my control. I'd had no thought of trying to get him to marry me.

I picked at my comforter, though of course, being a royal thing, it had no loose threads or raveled weave to pick at. *Why,* I wondered, *had telling Jed my story left me feeling so let down? Shouldn't I still feel triumphant, victorious?*

Hadn't I gotten what I wanted?

13

At dinner that night, the king announced a tournament to be held on the castle grounds. A flurry of excitement followed his words. Cyronna, who was seated on my right, clutched my arm and exclaimed, "Did you hear? Saturday afternoon? Oh, won't it be glorious?"

For once, I didn't find her enthusiasm cloying. Yes, it would be glorious. A tournament would have to be held outside. And obviously the entire royal court would be invited, or else the king wouldn't have announced it to one and all. So . . . fresh air! Sunshine! I cared naught about which horse won which race, which man won which wrestling bout. But the promise of getting out from under the castle roof for a few hours—that could keep my spirits up for days.

I all but sleepwalked through the rest of the week. Even my sessions with Jed, once the highlight of my days (but only because my time with the prince had to be chaperoned, making us awkward, I always reminded myself)—even that time seemed flat and dull compared with the prospect of going outdoors. Or maybe it was because Jed seemed different now, unusually distant and distracted.

"Is something wrong?" I finally asked him on Friday.

"No, no," he mumbled. "Just thinking about . . . uh . . . the war refugees."

He looked so hangdog, I tried to cheer him up by teasing, "Come on! It's springtime! Can you not take a vacation from worrying about the refugees? Or, how's this: Why not enter the tournament, and if you win something, maybe the king will be so impressed he'll give you whatever you want?"

Jed looked away, obviously not amused.

"I'm not good at that type of thing," he muttered.

My time with Jed was so unsatisfying, I tried to find the servant girl Mary later that day, hoping at least she would be willing to joke around with me. She always was. But when she scurried into my room upon my summons, she too looked distracted.

"I'm sorry, Princess," she burst out after a few seconds. "Can't we talk some other time? Mum has me polishing every trophy in the castle, so they can be displayed at the tournament, and do you know how many thousands of trophies they have just lying around this place?"

I was so lonely I almost said, "Can't you just bring them in here, and we can talk while you work?" But I could picture the horror on Madame Bisset's face if she came in the room while that was going on. She would be perfectly capable of dismissing Mary on the spot, and I knew from things Mary had said without meaning to, that her family couldn't survive without her income, small as it was.

Anyhow, I would feel strange, sitting idle while my friend worked beside me.

I resigned myself to feeling miserable the rest of the day. I wouldn't even get to see the prince, since he was entertaining a foreign delegation that had come to see the tournament.

But at least I had the tournament to look forward to.

Saturday dawned bright and fair. I could tell, even through the castle's tiny windows, that it was the kind of June day you spend winters dreaming about—warm and balmy, with gentle breezes carrying the first scent of summer flowers.

At eight o'clock, my maid showed up to dress me. Someone had decreed that I should wear some new-fangled fashion—or torture device, as I saw it—and the maid laced me tightly into what felt like a box on my torso. I'd worn corsets before, of course, but never like this steel-and-wood contraption. When she finished, I could barely breathe.

"Couldn't you . . . loosen . . . it . . . a little?" I managed to gasp.

The maid, one of the most hoity-toity I'd encountered, gave me a look of withering scorn.

"But, Princess. You used to be so slender."

I looked down to where my bosom was threatening to burst over the top of my too-tight dress. I had filled out some in the past weeks of sitting around doing nothing more strenuous than needlepoint, and eating food that was healthy and plentiful, even if it wasn't exactly to my taste. I'd thought it was good not to look so undernourished anymore.

"Just take this thing off me, okay?" I asked.

The maid's face set in an expression of downright defiance.

"I can't. Queen's orders."

"I can't believe the queen cares that much what I wear," I protested.

"She might not. But the prince does. He asked his mother to have you wear something that shows you off." Her voice was particularly mocking on the last three words. "And this is the latest fashion, just in. As the prince's betrothed, you should wear it first."

I felt light-headed. The prince and the queen weren't around to debate with, and in that dress, I could hardly dash out of the room demanding to see them. Should I fight with the maid? I couldn't take the dress off by myself. I decided to make the best of it. I took a shaky half breath that barely brought air into my lungs, and favored the maid with what I hoped was a dignified smile.

But I could hear Jed's words echoing in my head: "You took charge of your own destiny." What a joke. I couldn't even take charge of my own clothes.

It was a full hour before they summoned me. The ladies-in-waiting came down the hall, in dresses every bit as ridiculous as mine.

"Princess!" Simprianna purred. "Thank you—" She had to stop to take a shallow breath. "Thank you for bringing this wonderful fashion to our kingdom. These new corsets do"—another breath—"wonders for our figures."

She spun around and it was true, her waist looked no wider than a gold coin. It was amazing if you liked that kind of thing.

"I had nothing to do with it," I snapped. "And I have every intention of ending the fashion as soon as I can."

Madame Bisset appeared just in time to give me a reproving look.

"Princess! Ladies! We shan't keep the court waiting!"

She led us down the grand staircase, through the vast ballroom and out onto the castle lawns. The fresh air felt like a blessing against my face, and my sour mood began to ebb a bit.

In front of us, dozens of riders were lined up before the reviewing stand. They kept their hands down and their heads bowed, and even the horses stood perfectly still. They looked like a tableau or a tapestry, their lines and colors already preserved forever. But you could tell they all longed for movement and action; horses and riders alike wanted the formalities over so they could do what they loved.

The crier called out, "Princess Cynthiana Eleanora, Prince Charming's betrothed, and her royal attendants."

I heard polite applause from the stands. I wasn't sure if the court had so little enthusiasm for me or if they were just too well-bred to show more.

Madame Bisset led us to a section of the stands covered by a striped tent. I sat quickly in a padded chair in the middle, and the others followed my example. The chair was too low to afford me a good view of the tournament grounds, and I was just about to ask for a replacement when I saw Madame Bisset motioning to a servant, who promptly lowered the open side of the tent. Now we were surrounded on four sides by cloth walls. We could see nothing outside the tent except a half inch of sunlight at the bottom.

"What? What'd you do that for?" I squawked in surprise. "Now I can't see."

Simprianna turned to me in astonishment. "You thought they would make us watch the tournament?" She gave a shiver of revulsion. "Horses racing? Men fighting each other? Possibly even"—her face turned pale and she could barely whisper—"bleeding?"

I leaped from my chair, proud that I could leap in that insane dress. As it was, I had a second of fearing I would black out. I steadied myself and demanded, "Open that curtain this instant!"

The servant looked from me to Madame Bisset. She waved him away as though I had not spoken.

"Begone, James. Your services are no longer needed here."

When he had ducked out under the tent, she whipped her gaze toward me.

"You are a fool," she all but snarled. "You do not know our customs, and yet you try to change them."

I couldn't believe my ears.

"You mean, you go to the tournament and don't watch it? Why? Why not just stay locked in the castle, doing needlepoint forever?" Just then I noticed that several of the women had, indeed, pulled out embroidery. I laughed, almost hysterically. "Oh, I get it, it's a change of pace to do needlepoint in a cloth prison instead of a stone one—"

"Silence!" Madame Bisset hissed. "You are a disgrace to your gender. Do you not understand? You are here to beautify the tournament. And yet, if you were visible throughout, you would distract the riders and wrestlers. We will open the tent at the end, and you will present the ribbons."

I gasped.

"So we aren't allowed to see, because we might be seen."

"Correct."

I truly lost control then.

"The queen is out there watching. Are you saying she's too ugly to distract anyone?"

Madame Bisset glared.

"She is not a virgin," she whispered. Even in such a low tone, her voice still carried her full fury at being made to mention such a matter. "It is that combination of virginity and beauty that men must be protected from."

I couldn't stand to look at Madame Bisset another second. I appealed to the others.

"Why do you put up with this?" I asked. "Doesn't she make you want to scream?"

Every single one of them gazed at me blankly.

"Don't you ever want to do something—something real? Don't you ever get sick of being ladies-in-waiting? Have any of you ever wondered what you're waiting for?"

"That is what women do. We wait," Simprianna said primly. "Men go out and have adventures, and we wait for their return. They like to know that we are safe at home, waiting. And in this case, we also wait on you, dear Princess."

Her speech finished, Simprianna looked around to make sure her answer was correct.

I didn't wait to gauge anyone else's reaction. Thoroughly disgusted, I reached for the tent wall. I don't know if I intended to leave, or simply to pull back the cloth so I could see. But I was suffocating in the closed tent. I didn't think I could stand another second of it.

Just as I started to move the cloth, I felt a firm hand on my wrist. Madame Bisset stopped me with an unexpectedly strong grasp. She locked my arms together and whispered in my ear. "You open that tent, and you will never marry the prince. Never. You will be cast from the castle like so much refuse."

I did what was expected of me then. I fainted.

14

"You suffered too much sun at the tournament, Princess?" Mary asked me when she crept into my room that night.

I had been confined to my bed ever since the faint. And I do mean confined. Madame Bisset stayed in my chambers the whole time. She told everyone, "I must assure my precious charge doesn't exert herself unnecessarily." I believe she actually intended to berate me more as soon as I woke. So I feigned sleep until finally I heard her slip out the door at half past seven, murmuring, in the fakest voice I'd ever heard, "The poor dear is so exhausted after all the excitement. . . ."

Mary must have been spying on my room, because she slipped in as soon as Madame Bisset left.

"Of course I didn't suffer too much sun," I told Mary crankily. "What's too much sun? I barely saw a single ray of sunshine. It was that stupid dress. I couldn't breathe. Why would any-one wear that torture device?"

Mary patted my hand.

"But you looked so beautiful in it, Your Highness. I saw you across the field. . . ."

I snorted. "Oh, beauty. What's that good for?"

Mary stared, her eyes round.

"It won you the prince, did it not?"

I snorted again. I seemed to be trying to do everything I could to annoy Madame Bisset, even though she wasn't there.

"I prefer to think he was captivated by my charming personality." I giggled to let Mary know I was trying to make fun of myself. But Mary only looked away.

"What?" I asked.

"Nothing, Princess." Mary patted my hand again. "I should leave and let you rest."

"But I've been resting all day. I'm full of rest. I'm sick of it." I shoved back the covers and sprang from the bed. I hopped up and down on the cold floor. "I want to *do* something. Jump. Dance. Run. Live."

Mary hid a yawn, and I realized who truly did need the rest. She had probably been up at dawn and had worked constantly ever since. I remembered days like that, when all I wanted to do by nightfall was drop in a heap and not move until morning. She had probably had to drag herself in to see me. She was a true friend.

I sat down on the bed.

"Mary, are you tired?"

"A—" She yawned again, so hugely I heard her jaw crack. "A little."

"Then you should go to bed. Really. I'll be fine."

Her eyes were already half closed.

"All right."

But after she left, I paced the floor, so full of nervous energy I would have liked to scream too.

Up. Back. Up. Back. What was I going to do? I absolutely could not live the way everyone wanted me to. I would go mad.

Except—I remembered Madame Bisset's threat: "You open that tent, and you will never marry the prince." If I loved the prince, couldn't I adapt? Couldn't I change? Maybe I could get a little more freedom, force Madame Bisset and her cronies to bend some, after I was married and had some power. They could give a little, I could give a little. Surely it was worth it, for the sake of loving the prince.

I waited to be swept up in my usual rosy glow of love for Charm. I waited for my heart to speed up, the way it always did at the thought of him. I waited for the flush to creep up my face, the delicious shiver to crawl up my back.

Nothing happened.

I tested myself again.

Charm? Prince Charming? I conjured up the image of his perfect face, his perfect hair, his perfect body. I pictured him kissing me, touching me, holding me.

I felt nothing. Except—bored.

I paced faster, almost running, as if I could escape the thought I didn't want to think. It caught me anyway. I stood still, overcome with dread, knowing what I didn't want to know.

I didn't love Prince Charming.

15

The clock ticked. I watched the hands move, almost to eight, almost marking the time when the door would open and I'd see the prince for the first time since I'd—what? Fallen out of love with him? Realized I'd never loved him? Just plain gotten confused?

It had been two long days since the tournament and my fainting spell and my lonely, late-night realization. During those days, I'd debated again and again what I should do. I couldn't marry a man I didn't love, even if he was the prince. Especially if he was the prince. It wasn't fair. There were hundreds of girls in the kingdom who would love to marry him. How could I, the only girl who didn't want him, be the one he vowed to keep forever?

On the other hand, how could I back out now? The wedding was barely a month away. I tried to picture my mouth forming the words, "Prince, you must release me from our betrothal." I pictured the news spreading through the castle, the gossip throughout the kingdom. I told myself I didn't care about gossip. But what would I do then? What would the prince do? How could I hurt him like that?

What if I was wrong? What if I'd just had an off night, and I truly did love him after all?

I really, really, really hoped that was true. Surely seeing him again, in the flesh, would bring everything back. Surely I hadn't had a failure of love, only a failure of imagination.

The clock struck the first *Dong!* of eight and I jumped. Behind me the chaperon made a small sound—it could have been a dry laugh at my expense, or just a cough.

At the second *Dong!* I shifted my gaze to the prince's door. I held my breath, remembering to release it only when my eyesight began to blur. I had no intention of ever fainting again. This time I wouldn't even be able to blame it on my clothing. For once, I'd won a battle—no one had attempted to put one of the newfangled corsets on me since the tournament. See, see, I told myself, you shouldn't feel so trapped. You are in control of your own life.

The door opened, and there was the prince.

I put on what I hoped was a gracious smile, but inwardly I was frantic, checking my response. Heart rate? A little fast, but that seemed to be mainly because I was nervous. Flushed face? No. Shiver up the back? None.

The prince smiled back at me. He was breathtakingly handsome. Wasn't that enough?

He kissed my hand, and I felt only numbness.

"Prince—," I blurted. "Why did you fall in love with me? Why do you want to marry me?"

He blinked, my hand still caught in his.

"You're the most beautiful woman I've ever seen," he said.

I waited for a long time. Then I asked, "Is that all?"

He looked confused.

"You're so beautiful," he murmured again, and brushed a kiss against my cheek. I'd spent every previous moment with him longing for him to do that very thing. Tonight the kiss didn't move me.

"But—" I pulled away, ever so slightly. "What if I had an accident, and my face were hideously disfigured?"

"Oh, Princess," he laughed. "What do you ever do that could hurt you?"

It was true. Needlepointing was hardly likely to lead to facial scars.

"What if I got disgustingly fat?"

The prince laughed again.

"Is *that* what this is about? My dear, surely you've gained only a few pounds. I'm certain you'll lose them before the wedding. Madame Bisset told my mother she'd watch what you eat very carefully—"

"My weight is not a problem!" So many angry responses sprang to my tongue that I choked on my own words. I began coughing, and the prince gingerly patted me on the back. When I finally regained control, the prince took my hands again and peered soulfully into my eyes.

"You should not fret your pretty head about these matters," he said. "You are a princess."

But I'm not, I wanted to say. *I don't want to be.*

But was I sure?

I spent the next week biting my tongue. I wanted so badly to confide in somebody—anybody—that I even considered sneaking out of the castle and going to talk to Mrs. Branson, my next-door neighbor back in the village. But I didn't want to involve her, maybe getting her in trouble.

That was the same reason I had to watch what I said to Mary and Jed. And yet, they were my only possible sources of information. So I was like a spy, asking questions I didn't want to know the answer to, in hopes that they'd drop some tidbit I longed for.

"What do you think love is?" I asked Jed.

He got a dreamy look in his eye.

"Love is a wondrous thing. It moves mountains and stills a baby's cries. It beats inside every human's heart, yet is more precious than gold. It cannot be bought or sold or stolen. It keeps us alive."

I wondered why he looked sad when he turned his gaze back to me.

"Whom do you love?" I persisted.

"Oh, Princess, you do wander so from your lesson," he said with a laugh.

And because he'd called me "Princess," I knew that meant: subject closed. Lately, more and more subjects seemed to be closed with Jed.

I tried a different tack with Mary.

"How did people respond when they learned the prince was going to marry me?"

"Oh, la, Princess, as soon as they saw you, they understood," she answered as she dusted my mantel.

"That beauty thing again," I said sulkily. I looked at Mary carefully. "There was something you wouldn't tell me before. . . . Why does beauty matter so much?"

"Me mum says 'tis because men have eyes," Mary said stiffly. I saw that we were treading on dangerous territory. Mary was far from beautiful. I had to be wary lest I hurt her feelings. But I had to know.

"The prince seems especially concerned about it . . . ," I said.

"Surely you know—the Charmings must always have beautiful children. It's like the law or something."

"So it's more important to have a beautiful wife than a royal one."

Mary's expression didn't change, so I knew she'd known all along that I wasn't truly a princess. She waited so long to reply that I wondered what else she knew.

"It's so strange the way the prince picked me—just out of the crowd, at the ball . . . ," I said, watching Mary's face. She kept her head down, dusting a particularly crevice-filled stone in my wall.

"I heard the king's advisers talking, before the ball," she finally said. "They didn't know I was there, polishing the woodwork. Being ugly is like being invisible sometimes, you know? No—I guess you wouldn't know. Anyhow, they were talking about how the prince had to marry before he turned twenty-one, but none of the eligible princesses met all the requirements for beauty. So one of them decided to have a ball, for everyone, and they would rate all the women and pick the best one for the prince."

I remembered the setup at the ball, with some women sent into one ballroom, some into another. Had the less attractive ones been shunted away? For once, I felt a pang of compassion for Griselda and Corimunde. I remembered the way I'd been announced, as though I were a beauty contestant. Wait—I had been a beauty contestant. And the prince had been the prize.

"So he didn't even choose me. He just did what he was told," I muttered. "He wasn't in love with me. He isn't."

Mary gave her dust cloth an extra-vigorous shake.

"The prince isn't really smart enough to know how to fall in love, is he?" she quipped. "He wouldn't know how to get out of bed in the morning if he didn't have advisers telling him which foot to put on the floor first."

Immediately, Mary got a stricken look on her face and clapped her hand over her mouth.

"Oh, Princess, I'm sorry. I forgot who I was talking to. I was thinking about what we say below-quarters. That's just . . . servants' talk. You know how servants talk."

Yes, I knew how servants talked. They told the truth when no one else would.

I waited for anger to sweep over me—not at Mary, but at the prince and his royal advisers. Or even at myself, for not understanding the contest I'd unwittingly entered. But no anger came. Instead, I felt relieved.

If the prince didn't really love me, then it was okay that I didn't love him. It was okay if I broke our engagement.

I could escape.

16

I wasn't hasty. I waited a week, trying to figure out how I'd tell the prince I didn't want to marry him. But it wasn't easy to hold my tongue.

On Monday, Madame Bisset told me that I was to begin having fittings for my wedding gown every morning, instead of once a week.

"But—" I started to protest. I stopped in time, remembering I couldn't call off the wedding gown fittings before I called off the wedding. And no matter how much I felt like screaming from the rooftops, "I'm not going through with this! I'm getting out of here!" I owed it to the prince to tell him first, not Madame Bisset.

Madame Bisset continued talking, as if whatever I might say was beneath her notice.

"The fittings will take the place of your religion lessons," she announced.

I felt panicked. If I had no religion lessons, when would I ever get a chance to talk to Jed?

"So a dress is more important than religion?" I asked.

Madame Bisset only looked at me.

"I'm sure that you've hardly been getting quite the caliber of instruction you need since His Excellency, the Lord Reston, ah, took ill," she said. "If you're so interested in the subject, perhaps you can continue lessons after the wedding, when he recovers his health."

I was glad to hear someone thought he might recover. But I couldn't stand the insult to Jed.

"Jed's a wonderful teacher!" I proclaimed fiercely.

"I meant no offense to the young *Lord* Reston," Madame Bisset said. "But he's not his father."

No, thank God, I thought. Still, as ridiculous as Madame Bisset's reasoning was, I felt a slight moment of relief at not seeing Jed. If I continued having lessons with him, I'd be too tempted to confide in him, to ask his advice about how to break the news to the prince—and about what to do when I left the castle. And those were things I needed to figure out on my own. So far I was sure only that I couldn't hurt the prince, and I couldn't go back to living with Lucille.

I wondered, that week, that nobody said to me, "Princess, you're very quiet. What's on your mind?" But nobody seemed to notice that I moved through the days like an automaton, without feeling, without thought. Maybe that was all they'd ever expected of me. I stood like a statue every morning while yards of satin and lace were pinned around me. I sat like a porcelain doll every afternoon while the royal hairdresser piled curls atop my head and combed and brushed and braided until my hair looked more like a woven basket than real hair. I smiled like a fool every evening while the ministers and officials around me pontificated about the Sualan War.

I paid attention only during my every-other-night meetings with the prince—and then, all I could think about was how much he repulsed me. How had I ever thought I'd loved him? Now when I looked into those perfect blue eyes, I saw only the vacancy behind them. Had he ever had a thought in his entire life? I'd even give him credit for the dull ones, like, *I think I'll wear my blue waistcoat instead of the green one today.* But no, he even had people to pick out his clothes for him.

Now that I no longer made an effort to talk, we mostly sat in silence.

"Good evening, Princess," he'd say.

"Good evening, Your Highness," I'd say.

And then there was a half hour filled with nothing but an occasional "You're so beautiful" from the prince.

I came to hate those words.

Now? I'd think. *Do I tell him now?*

The sentences ran through my head: "Your Highness, I—"

"Prince, I—"

"Look, unCharming, I can't stand you, and there's no way I'm going to marry you!"

I held my tongue and kept practicing in my head. I wasn't ready yet. I vowed that even if I did only one thing with grace and dignity my whole time in the castle, this would be it.

17

The clock struck eight. The candles flickered. The prince opened the door and came to sit next to me. He kissed my hand, and I had to concentrate on not recoiling.

But after tonight, I wouldn't have to pretend anymore. It was time to tell.

"Your Majesty," I began. "I have been thinking—"

He chuckled.

"Always a dangerous thing for a woman to do," he said. "Especially one as beautiful as you."

I reconsidered my desire to break the news gently. He deserved to be slugged. I raised my chin and decided to be nice anyway.

"I—I know you won't like hearing this, but I must tell you. I can't marry you."

I held my breath and watched the prince carefully. His expression didn't change. My words didn't seem to register.

"What?" he asked.

"I want to call off the wedding. I can't marry you. I, well, I'm very sorry, but I just don't love you. I thought I did, but it was just infatuation, I guess. I honestly don't even know you—"

The prince clapped his hand over my mouth. He made no effort to be gentle. It hurt. Then he turned and spoke over my shoulder.

"Jeedens," he hollered at the chaperon behind us.

"Wha-what? What do you wish, Your Majesty?" The ancient servant jerked to attention. From his flustered demeanor, I could tell he hadn't heard what I'd said. Perhaps even he had found the conversations between the prince and me too boring to listen to. I saw his eyes take in the sight of the prince holding his hand over my mouth and then, as if a curtain fell across his vision, I could practically see him making the decision not to notice. No wonder he'd managed to stay in service to the royal family for so long.

"You may leave now," the prince commanded.

"Yes, Your Highness. Yes, Your Majesty." Jeedens gathered up his robes, but stood for a moment looking confused.

"Go back to your room," the prince said. "You are dismissed."

Only when Jeedens had scrambled out the door did the prince release his grip on my face.

"You can do that?" I asked in amazement. "Dismiss the chaperon—just like that?"

"I'm the prince," Charming said.

"But aren't we breaking some rule, being together alone?" I persisted.

Prince Charming shrugged.

"I'm the prince," he repeated. "My family makes the rules. We don't have to follow them if we don't want to."

I wished I'd known weeks ago that we didn't have to be chaperoned. I remembered my old daydreams: The prince and I, alone together, cuddling and whispering. Intimate. Maybe if we'd had that from the beginning, I wouldn't be breaking the engagement now. Maybe . . . I looked at the prince carefully. His stunning blue eyes looked only cold and empty to me now. If we'd had intimate conversations from the beginning, I probably would have wised up and broken the engagement sooner. Or never agreed to be married in the first place.

I rubbed my face where he'd gripped too tight. The prince crossed the room and made sure the door was closed.

"Anyhow," I said when he turned around, "I don't want to cause a scene or make problems or hurt you—but I don't think marriage is a good idea for us. You can have your pick of girls, and you deserve one who will love you. One you love."

The prince stared at me.

"What are you talking about? You're my betrothed. You *will* marry me."

"No," I said. "I will not."

The prince stood still, looking puzzled. As masterful as he'd been with Jeedens, he didn't seem to know how to deal with me. He came over and clutched my shoulders.

"Don't ever say that again!" he commanded with an emphatic shake.

"Whether I say it again or not, 'tis no matter," I said defiantly, pulling back from his grasp. "The fact is, I don't want to marry you, and I don't see why you would want to marry someone who doesn't want to marry you—"

"Stop it!" the prince shouted. "Stop it! Stop it! Stop it!"

I was put in mind of a three-year-old throwing a temper tantrum. The prince might as well have been holding his hands over his ears and chanting, "I can't hear you. I can't hear you. . . ." Thinking of the prince as a child only irked me more.

"Look," I said, standing up. "I wanted to handle this in a . . . in an adult manner. But under the circumstances, perhaps it would be best if I just left. I'm sorry things didn't work out differently."

I began walking toward the door. The prince caught me halfway across the floor. He grabbed my waist from behind.

"No!" he screamed. "You can't!"

I still had some thoughts of dignity. I didn't struggle.

"Let go of me," I said, ice dripping from every word.

He whirled me around so forcefully, I stumbled and landed on the floor.

"Get on the couch," he panted, looking frantically from me to the door. "Sit on the couch. Stay there."

I stood up. I should have known better, but I blurted, "You can't make me."

The prince's frenzy increased. His eyes darted around the room.

"You have to!" he insisted. "As prince of the land, I

command you to stay on that couch until I return."

I started walking toward the door. The prince looked stunned, as if no one had ever disobeyed him before. He pushed me back onto the couch, holding me there with the weight of his body. "Just—until—I—can—find—some-one—to—tell—me—what—to—do," he muttered through clenched teeth.

That did it. I might have continued trying to appeal to reason—what little he had. I would gladly have sat still to discuss the matter between us. But it infuriated me that he had to ask someone else how to accept my refusal.

"Get away from me!" I yelled, trying to shove him back.

He pushed me down again. Soon we were fighting as shamelessly as two ragamuffin boys vying for a crust of bread in some back alley. The prince did not defend him-self well. Even as I punched him in the stomach, he protested, "You can't do that! Princesses don't— Ladies don't—"

I managed to extricate myself from his hold, but as I slipped away, he grabbed at my skirt. I heard the fabric give way. I turned around to see that he held a long strip of one of the ruffles of my petticoat. He held the fabric up in the air, and both of us stared at it in shock. I felt a jolt of shame. How could things have turned so ugly? I looked at the prince, wondering if he had the same thought. Maybe we could laugh about this, and resolve everything that way. But the prince kept his eyes on the torn cloth. His expression changed. I swear I saw the idea occur to him; the look of craftiness traveled over his face so slowly

it was like watching a sunrise. I could have escaped then, while he was thinking, but I was too intrigued by the notion that the prince might be having his very first original thought. What would it be?

And then, when it was too late for me to react, the prince reached out and wrapped the fabric around my wrists, knotting it tightly. When I started to protest, he tore off another ruffle and tied it around my mouth. I struggled, but the prince was far stronger than me, and now he was determined too. In seconds, he had my ankles bound together as well.

And then he left, latching the door firmly behind him.

18

For a long time after he left, I couldn't seem to comprehend what had happened. We had fought. Prince Charming had tied me up. How could that be?

I leaned my head back and closed my eyes, my mind a jumble. *So much for breaking it off gently,* I thought. The humor helped my mind clear, but I couldn't laugh. What would happen next?

I listened for footsteps in the hall outside, but there were none. He wasn't coming back. But no one else was coming to rescue me either.

"Help?" I tried to scream, experimentally, but the gag was so effective, I could barely hear myself.

Well, it might have been the wrong person who heard you anyhow, I thought. I looked down, taking stock. The ties were cutting into my wrists and ankles, and one of my knuckles was bleeding. Probably I'd scraped it hitting the prince. But if that was my worst injury, I was still capable of rescuing myself.

I sat up and managed to push myself off the couch into a standing position. I could feel the blood rushing from my head, and I swayed—dangerously so, considering that my ankles were tied tightly together. But I stood my ground and felt steady again in a moment.

The door was almost twelve feet away, but I was certainly capable of hopping that far. I'd figure out what to do about the latch when I got there. I bent my knees and sprang up—once, twice. . . . On the third hop I landed on my ripped petticoat and went sprawling across the floor. I was struggling to get back up when the door opened.

"Princess—" It was Madame Bisset.

I winced.

"I know, I know," I muttered. "Very unladylike." Of course she couldn't hear me through the gag.

Madame Bisset turned, and the prince and one of his advisers followed her in. I'd seen the adviser before at dinners. He was a sturdy, sensible-looking fellow named Twelling, who always seemed to bring up more practical points than any of the others. I dared to have hope.

Twelling and the prince scooped me off the floor and set me on the couch. Neither they nor Madame Bisset sat beside me. But Twelling gently removed the gag.

"My hands and feet are tied too," I reminded him.

Twelling had the grace to look embarrassed.

"I'm aware of that," he said. "But we need to . . . settle this first. I understand you and the prince had a lovers' spat?"

His choice of words astounded me.

"It was a lovers' spat," I said carefully, "the way the Sualan War is a friendly disagreement."

"Ah, yes. Well—" Twelling cleared his throat. "I see that things got a little out of hand. But you are the prince's intended, and he loves you, and when you made your little threat about the wedding, well, of course he felt a little panicky. Now, just what is it that you hoped to gain? A grander dress? More of your family invited to the wedding? Different food at the wedding banquet?"

I swallowed hard, struggling to be diplomatic.

"The prince must not have understood," I said. "I'm not trying to gain anything. I want exactly what I said I want—to cancel the wedding. I don't want to marry him. I didn't an hour ago, and I certainly don't now."

So much for diplomacy.

"But you see . . ." Twelling bent down and actually patted my hand. "What you want isn't, ah, isn't *possible*. Do you understand that word?"

I was too insulted to nod.

"You see, no one can call off a wedding to a prince. Especially not to a Charming. It just isn't done."

"I'm doing it," I said.

"You little—" Madame Bisset stepped forward. Twelling gave her a meaningful look. She ran her tongue over her lips. "I mean, my dear princess. I don't know what prompted this, but surely you aren't in your right mind. You haven't been yourself since the tournament." Madame Bisset looked right and left, at Twelling and the prince. "She fainted. Perhaps she was too embarrassed to mention it to you, Your Highness, but she was unable to leave her bed for the rest of the day."

"Only because you did everything but tie me down!" I protested. "If the prince had been there, maybe he could have taken care of it for you."

The prince moved toward me, complaining, "See, that's the kind of thing she—" Twelling laid a warning hand on his arm. The prince stepped back and shut up.

Twelling and Madame Bisset exchanged looks. Twelling cleared his throat yet again. I decided that that could get to be a very annoying habit.

"Well, we do have a dilemma here, don't we?" Twelling asked rhetorically.

"No," I said. "There's an easy solution. Just let me go. Cancel the wedding, have another ball, and pick someone else to bear your precious, *beautiful* children."

Twelling frowned. He pulled Madame Bisset and the prince to the side, and they conferred in whispers. I heard only scattered words: ". . . the humiliation . . ." ". . . family history of instability . . ." ". . . but will it work?" The prince didn't seem to be saying much. I remembered Mary's witticism about him: "He wouldn't know how to get out of bed in the morning if he didn't have advisers telling him which foot to put on the floor first." What kind of a fool had nothing to say about whether or not he was going to marry someone who'd rejected him? Shame washed over me. I had little room to make fun of him. How intelligent had I been, agreeing to marry him in the first place?

After nearly a quarter hour of whispering, Twelling

strode to the door and left briefly. Madame Bisset and the prince were silent in his absence. When he returned, the three of them spoke only a few seconds before returning to my side. The prince and Twelling hung back. Obviously Madame Bisset had been selected to speak for all of them.

"Princess," she said in a deceptively soothing tone. "It is clear what's happened here."

I waited. She cleared her throat. Was Twelling's bad habit contagious?

"You have been under a great deal of strain, adapting to castle life," she said. "Perhaps those of us teaching you have been at fault, for failing to realize just what a delicate creature you are."

Delicate? I'd like to see Madame Bisset try to carry the sixteen buckets of water it always took to fill Corimunde and Griselda's bathing tub. I'd like to see her haul fifty-pound bags of potatoes home from the market, without stopping once to rest. I'd like to see her scrub and clean from dawn until midnight with no food but a bowl of porridge. I was so busy trying to think of the exact right example to prove that delicacy was not my problem that I almost missed her next words.

"We—your beloved prince, Sir Twelling, and I—we want to ensure that you return to your former health and vigor. When you do, I'm sure you'll realize the error of your ways, and thank us for not indulging your foolishness. . . ."

She patted my arm. Something stung my skin, and for a second I was distracted, puzzling whether I'd been pinched by her ring or—surely not!—a less-than-perfectly

manicured nail. I couldn't focus on her next words. Then I couldn't focus on her face.

But I did catch one last glimpse of her malicious smile before I slid into darkness.

19

I woke feeling woozy-headed, stiff, cold, and sore. I had a moment of wondering if I'd merely had a strange dream about living in a castle—I always woke stiff and cold and sore back home. But then I opened my eyes and saw the uneven stone of the castle, instead of the plaster walls of home. No, the dream was true. Only it had become a nightmare.

I sat up slowly, fighting waves of dizziness. When I finally reached an upright position, I leaned my head against the wall behind me and surveyed my surroundings. I was alone. But I was not in my usual room. This place was nothing but stone walls, dirt floor, and the narrow wooden bench I'd been lying on. The only window was high over my head. It held no glass to keep out the chill—only a crisscross of bars. The heavy wooden door across from me also was barred, and lined with heavy rods of iron.

Though I'd never been here before, I knew where I was.

The dungeon.

I blinked several times, as if hoping the view would change if I only looked again.

"I don't understand," I murmured. "Why am I here?"

I thought back over everything that had happened, wondering if I'd missed some important clue. The prince had pushed me around and tied me up, certainly, but I didn't take him for a sadist. Just a dullard who'd never been told no before. As for Twelling and Madame Bisset, they were diabolical, but not crazy.

"How is *this* supposed to make me love the prince?" I asked out loud.

I raised my head, weakly, as though I could look out the prison bars for an answer. But the effort was a little too much for me, and my head clunked back against the wall. Pain shot through my whole body, and tears sprang to my eyes. And suddenly I understood. They didn't care about making me love the prince. They just wanted to break my spirit.

I drew my legs in and huddled on the bench, weeping silently. When I had to, I wiped my nose on my sleeve, because there was nothing else.

What a fool I'd been. What had I expected the prince to say? "Oh, that's okay, El. I understand. You go on with your life, and I'll go on with mine. No hard feelings." I knew better than that. Hadn't I seen love affairs go sour in the village? When the wife of Rosten, the pig-tender, got mad at him, she'd burned every one of his leather vests and cursed him by sticking pins in a dozen pigs' eyes. For all their prissy manners and French accents, the people in the castle were no better than a pig-tender's wife. Just better dressed.

And more powerful. I shivered, remembering something I'd read in a book of my father's, long ago. It was about a king in another land and another time, who'd had his wives beheaded when he lost interest in them.

Why hadn't I remembered that sooner?

Had I gotten too accustomed to having people fawn over me? "Oh, Princess, you're so beautiful." "Oh, Princess, your hair curls so perfectly." "Oh, Princess, you'll make the loveliest bride. . . ." Had I actually believed all that? Could I think of a single person in the whole castle who truly liked me, who wasn't just kissing up because they thought I would someday be queen?

Yes, I could. I could even think of two. Mary and Jed.

I felt the first stirring of hope, but it died quickly. Okay, so not everybody hated me. So what? What could Mary or Jed do? Mary was just a servant girl, and Jed—I swallowed hard, forcing myself to evaluate Jed as harshly as I'd evaluated myself. Jed wasn't a doer. He was a thinker, someone who cared about ideas and cared about doing right, but spent all his time pondering concepts like good and evil, instead of taking action. If I'd been him, caring as passionately as he did about the Sualan War victims, I would have found some way to help them. But Jed just sat and waited, wringing his hands and bemoaning the palace indifference.

He wouldn't be able to help me either.

I buried my face in my hands, not able to bear looking

at the dungeon around me a second longer. Why hadn't I just run away when I'd had the chance? If I'd been so concerned about not hurting the prince, I could have left a note.

"Princess?"

It was Madame Bisset. I evaluated my chances based on her one word. If she was still calling me "Princess," that was a good sign. They must still have hopes that I would consent to marry the prince. Or that I could be forced to. They weren't going to kill me.

I deliberately did not raise my head. If Madame Bisset thought I was still unconscious, perhaps I could overpower her when she came into my cell. She was taller and heavier than me, but she led a soft life in the palace, and I still had some muscles left from all those years of carrying cinders.

Madame Bisset didn't open the door.

"Princess, I know you're awake, so there's no use pretending," she said from the other side of the bars. "Just listen."

Her words were blunter and rougher than I'd ever heard from her before. Perhaps even she realized how ridiculous her faky, Frenchified, decorous talk would sound in the dungeon.

"You're going to stay here until you realize you have only one choice," she said. "And then you'll marry the prince."

I raised my head and yelled as forcefully as I could, "Never!"

I'd intended to keep giving her the silent treatment, which had always been so effective at infuriating Lucille. But, really, defiance was much more my style.

Madame Bisset wasn't fazed.

"Oh, yes. We'll keep you in the dungeon until the wedding day, if necessary."

I laughed, to show that she didn't scare me. But it was hard keeping my laughter from sliding into hysteria.

"Sure," I said sarcastically. "Prison pallor will look great with that beautiful gown."

Madame Bisset smiled.

"You'll look radiant," she said, almost reverently. "So thin, so pale."

She was right, I thought—they really did want me to look as if I'd spent my life in prison. Maybe that was how I'd won the prince in the first place, because I was so pale from staying in the house all day being Lucille's slave, so thin from never getting enough to eat. If it didn't affect me, I could feel plenty amused by the palace ideal of female beauty.

But it did affect me. It was the reason I was in the dungeon.

"Fine. I'm stuck here. I guess someone will bring me something to eat. Every once in a while," I said wildly. "I guess the only other thing I need to know is—where do I pee?"

I meant to shock her, using the common term for a bodily function that was too base to mention even with a euphemism. But Madame Bisset didn't flinch.

"There's a hole in the corner," she said. "You may squat."

She pointed through the bars, and for the first time I saw the dark depression beyond the other end of my bench. I peered over at it until the smell overwhelmed me. Obviously I wasn't the first prisoner who'd been held in this cell. Evidently the Charmings weren't as charming as they'd like their subjects to believe.

"Lucky me," I said. "I have all the amenities."

Madame Bisset sniffed.

"You," she said, "are a fool. Don't you know what you're throwing away? Maybe you think I'm like everyone else, castle born and castle bred. You've had no reason to think otherwise. But no—I'm like you. I was not born to nobility. I had to fight for everything I've gotten. I had to work. And I don't have a single regret about anything I had to do."

I regarded Madame Bisset for the first time as a potentially interesting person. What exactly had she had to do? Somehow, I didn't think she would tell me.

"What is wrong with you?" she ranted. "You know what it's like to be a commoner. They live in manure. They *are* manure! Why would you want to go back to that?"

"I just want to be free," I whispered.

"Free!" Madame Bisset practically spat out the word. "What's that? There's no such thing! Everything has a price. And I'm not paying the price for you. I'm not going to have everything I've worked for taken away by a ninny like you!"

I squinted, puzzled. Did she mean that her fate was somehow tied up with mine? Would she be blamed if I didn't shape up, marry the prince, and act like a proper princess? I didn't know what to think about those possibilities.

"I will come and see you every day," Madame Bisset said, a little more calmly. "And when you are ready, I will tell the guards to release you. Until then—"

She thrust a bowl through the bars and waited until I stumbled across the floor to take it. It was filled with a thin gruel. I thought at first that there were small chunks of meat floating on the surface, but they turned out to be weevils.

Madame Bisset was watching my reaction, so I was careful to keep my face expressionless.

"Good day," Madame Bisset said as she turned to leave.

"Good day to you as well," I said stiffly.

I watched through the bars until she was out of sight. Then I sat down and ate the gruel. I forced myself not to gag on the weevils.

"You can go ask Lucille," I whispered, though Madame Bisset was long gone. "It takes more than this to break me."

I hoped.

20

I had fallen into a fitful sleep on the bench that night when I heard the scratching at my door. *Mice,* I thought. *Or rats. It figures.* But then there was a whisper. "Princess? Are you in there?"

Gratefully I sprang to the door. "Mary? Is that you?"

"Aye. I followed Madame Bisset to find you, and I couldn't believe . . . Why are you here?"

"Take your pick of reasons. Either I'm testing the effect of cold, clammy dungeons on princesses' complexions, or I told the prince I didn't want to marry him."

Mary gasped, unaffected by my attempt at humor.

"You didn't," she said. "Didn't you know—I mean, why didn't you tell me you were going to do that? I could have—I mean—"

"Go ahead and say it," I said glumly. "You could have told me it'd land me here."

So I'd been a fool too for not confiding in anyone. Mary and Jed both would have told me the right way to break up with a prince: run like crazy. Well, there was still time for that.

"Mary, can you find Jed and get him to help me? Maybe you two can figure out some way to smuggle me out of here. Or maybe he can talk to the prince and everyone and convince them to set me free. He'll know. He'll know the best thing to do."

There was a long silence on the other side of the door. Then Mary spoke hesitantly.

"Princess, Master Reston is . . . is gone." For a minute, I feared that Jed had been punished somehow because of what I'd done. Surely no one realized that I was closer to him than any of my other instructors. Did they?

Mary went on.

"He left for the Sualan front today. I listened at a couple of doors—something about helping some folks who used to live where the battlefields are now. He had to leave in a big hurry."

So they'd given him his dearest wish. Somehow I had to think it was connected to me. Did they realize that he, at least, wouldn't advise the prince to keep me locked in a dungeon? I felt a little hurt that he hadn't tried to see me, to say good-bye. He'd gotten what he wanted, thanks to me. I guess that was all he cared about.

"But I can try to help you," Mary said in a quavery voice.

Her words echoed a little off the stone walls. In the dark, unable to see her face, I somehow understood the depths of her loyalty as I hadn't before. She was taking enormous risks, just coming to see me. I didn't feel worthy of her devotion. I tried to think of a gentle way to tell her there was nothing she could do for me.

"Mary, I appreciate your offer. Believe me," I said. "But—"

"But your fairy godmother's coming to get you?" she asked eagerly.

I bit my lip to hold back a sarcastic retort. Wouldn't the old lady have shown up before now if she existed?

"Mary, I don't have a fairy godmother," I said. "All those stories you heard were just made up."

"Then how did you get to be a princess?" Mary asked, puzzled.

"It was all my own foolishness," I said. "My own fault."

We sat in silence for a few minutes, Mary apparently trying to understand my magicless life, me feeling torn between wanting to send her away—for her own good— and wanting to stall her some more so that at least I wouldn't be left alone again. I kicked idly at a pebble on the ground. It skittered across the floor and landed with a plop, far down in the hole I'd been using in lieu of a chamber pot. I gasped, suddenly struck by an idea.

"Mary," I said urgently. "How close is the dungeon to the castle walls?"

I heard the rustle of her shrugging. "Couple of feet, give or take," she said. "Are you thinking of climbing out? You couldn't fit through the bars—"

"No, no," I said impatiently. "I want to dig. Can you get me a shovel? From the stable, maybe?"

"From the stable?" Even in a whisper, her voice carried a full load of puzzlement. "I guess."

"Good," I said. "Then do it. Please."

"Someone will see where you've dug," she protested. "You can't dig the whole way in one night, and then come day—"

"They won't see," I said. "I'm going to dig my way out through the crap hole."

21

Mary wasted a lot of time protesting that, as a princess, I couldn't go near a spot where anyone else had performed bodily eliminations. I tried to explain how many chamber pots I'd carried out and cleaned for Corimunde and Griselda and Lucille, but Mary was still too stunned by my lack of a fairy godmother to absorb what I was saying.

All the same, she was an obedient soul, and by the time the palace clock rang midnight—the fateful hour once again!—she had left and returned with a heavy shovel. Even with the smell of the crap hole, I still recoiled from the odor of the shovel as Mary handed it through the barred window in the door. I knew the dried mud I knocked off the handle had to be manure.

I reminded myself this was no time for all that delicacy training to kick in.

"It's stolen," Mary said hesitantly.

I took her meaning.

"I'll hide it by daylight," I promised. "I won't get you in trouble."

"I wish I could do the digging for you," she said wistfully.

"So do I," I joked. Mary didn't laugh. "But it's fitting—I got myself into this mess, so I've got to get myself out. Now, I'd love the company, but it's not safe for you to stay. And don't you need sleep?"

"Aye," she murmured. "I'll come back when I can."

As soon as I'd sent Mary away, I took a deep breath of relatively fresh air and lowered myself into the hole. I left the shovel on the dirt floor until I was down several feet, my knees braced against the sides of the hole. The stench was overwhelming. At first I held my breath, but I started feeling light-headed even as I reached back for the shovel. That wouldn't do. I gave up and inhaled deeply. After a few moments—when I figured I had become one with the smell—it stopped bothering me.

Awkwardly, I pulled the shovel down into the hole with me. The trick would be to dig far down enough on the side of the hole that the floor wouldn't collapse on my tunnel, but not so low that I'd lose a lot of time digging up to the surface once I reached the other side of the castle walls. I picked a spot about three feet down and poked the tip of the shovel into the packed earth. The shovel's handle was too long to fit straight across the hole, so I had to hold it at an awkward angle. Pushing with all my might, I managed to dislodge two pebbles and a sprinkling of dust. That wouldn't do.

I tried every other angle possible—even shimmying up the hole and bending over with the shovel below my feet.

But all I accomplished was to give myself severe back cramps. I climbed out of the hole to recover and think.

Me and my bright ideas. I heard the clock strike one, and I wondered if I might be better served by trying to get a good night's sleep so I'd have my wits about me when I saw Madame Bisset the next day. Could I somehow make her an ally, talk her into helping me escape? In the dark I pictured her face, the prim set of her lips, the upward tilt of her nose, the coldness of her eyes. No, she'd never be on my side. I'd do better pretending to cave in, just so they'd let me out of the dungeon. And then I could escape, once they no longer watched me so carefully.

Except they'd probably never stop watching me so carefully. I tried to imagine the rest of my life, always under guard, like a bird in a gilded cage. I couldn't live like that. I couldn't even pretend to want to live like that. The shovel was my only hope. If only the handle weren't so long—

With the speed of tinder catching fire, I realized my stupidity. *Okay, Ella, the handle's too long? So break it!*

I slammed it against my knee, and it split in two with a satisfying clunk.

I climbed back into the hole wondering how stupid I would have become if I'd stayed a princess much longer. Maybe that was the problem with everyone in the castle. Their lives were so soft and dull, they never had to think. Maybe under different circumstances Prince Charming would be designing buildings, writing books, speaking sixteen different languages. Maybe even my most vapid lady-in-waiting, Simprianna, was secretly capable of great genius.

That was such a laughable thought that I had extra energy thrusting the shovel back into the wall of the hole. This time I got out four pebbles and a clod of dirt the size of an apple.

At least this was an improvement.

I worked steadily the rest of the night, stopping to rest only once an hour, when I heard the palace clock chime. I told myself my goal that first night was only to make a big enough tunnel to hide the shovel in. But I reached that milestone at three o'clock, and mustered up the will to keep going. Madame Bisset had threatened to keep me in the dungeon until the wedding date, which was now just two weeks away. I was confident of my ability to dig myself out before that. But what if her threat was just a threat? What if they took pity on me and moved me back to my usual room after a few days? That certainly had nicer accommodations, but it was still a prison. And I didn't know how to escape from there.

As daybreak approached I began to fear that a guard or Madame Bisset might show up to check on me in the early morn. When I heard the five o'clock chiming, I pushed my shovel as far back into my tunnel as it would go and carefully climbed out of the hole for the day. My arms and shoulders ached, and my legs had long ago gone numb. I barely managed to stumble over to the plank bed. I believe I was asleep before the final *dong* of five.

22

My cell was still dim when Madame Bisset's voice woke me.

"So, sloth is among the faults we must cure in you," she jeered. "Are you worth the effort?"

Sleep startled, I was at a loss for dealing with this new, coarsened Madame Bisset. I held my tongue but sat up dizzily. My head ached and, once I began to move, so did every muscle in my body.

"What—what time is it?" I asked.

"High noon," she all but cackled. "Don't you see the lovely sunshine coming in the window?"

I refrained from pointing out that whatever lovely sunshine there might be outdoors would never venture into the dungeon—or anywhere else in the castle, for that matter.

"Did you get enough beauty rest?" she continued.

I decided an attempt at dignity would serve me well today. I didn't have enough energy for defiance.

"Yes, thank you," I said.

I heard slow, pounding footsteps coming down the hallway behind her. They put me in mind of hideous fairy tale giants, the kind that chant "Fee-fi-fo-fum" and brag about smelling blood. The man who appeared outside my barred window fit the image. He towered over Madame Bisset by at least a foot and a half. His clothes were filthy and torn, his hair and beard were a mass of tangles, and his leer was the most lecherous I'd ever seen. For the first time, I was glad of the heavy door of my cell.

"If I may introduce you to your jailer," Madame Bisset said, her perfect accent and primness returned. I didn't miss the point: She considered this brute more worthy of her manners than I was. "Princess Cynthiana Eleanora, this is Quog. Quog, Princess Cynthiana Eleanora."

Quog drooled.

"Heh," he rumbled.

"Pleased to meet you," I said, determined to match Madame Bisset in this pretense.

"Quog has been instructed to take very good care of you until the wedding," Madame Bisset said.

"And after?" I asked boldly.

Madame Bisset raised one eyebrow.

"If there is an after— If you prove to be unreformable and are still here, then— Quog has been told your fate is entirely in his hands. He may do as he wishes."

I wished I hadn't asked.

"Heh," Quog said again. "Heh-heh."

He panted like a dog begging for a treat.

"I want," he grunted. "That." He pointed at me.

"You're trying to scare me," I said to Madame Bisset. "It won't work." But against my will, an edge of fear crept into my voice.

Madame Bisset only smiled at me.

"Not now," she told Quog. "For today, just give her her gruel."

He slid a bowl through a space in the bars. Reluctantly, I stepped forward and tried to take it from him. But as soon as I was in reach, he grabbed my hand. His skin was leathery but strangely moist. I struggled to pull away, but he was too strong for me.

"No," Madame Bisset said forcefully. "Not today, Quog. You must let go."

Quog looked from me to her. He moaned like a scolded dog.

"Awww—" But he dropped my hand.

My bowl of gruel turned upside down on the floor.

"Too bad," Madame Bisset said. "That was your only meal today."

At the moment I didn't care. I rubbed my hand where Quog had touched me. I longed to go scrub it, he was that disgusting.

"Quog, you are dismissed," Madame Bisset said.

When he had lurched away, she leaned close and said, "Quog doesn't have a key to your cell. Yet."

I made myself stop rubbing my hand.

"Maybe—" I gulped. "Maybe it's just his appearance that's revolting. Maybe he's truly a very good person."

Madame Bisset laughed as if I'd told the world's funniest joke.

"No," she said cheerfully. "He's revolting through and through. Now, I must be going. Will you return with me?"

"Return to what?" I asked cautiously.

"Your rightful place," she said. "I believe the dressmaker would like you to try on your wedding gown again."

"Then I'll stay right here," I said.

"I hope you enjoy Quog's company," she said lightly, and turned and left.

Her departure must have been Quog's cue. The rest of the day he lingered outside my cell, alternating "heh's" and "I want's." Once, I decided to test my theory.

"Quog," I asked. "Did you have a happy childhood?"

"No," he said. "Wanted women. Couldn't get them. Now big. Get what want. Heh."

I lay down on my plank and closed my eyes, deciding to ignore him.

The next few days I did my best to sleep all day, to have energy to work all night. Each shovelful of dirt I removed and dropped down the crap hole carried Quog's face on it for me. I worked like a madwoman, without breaks. I tried to calculate how many more "heh-heh's" I'd have to endure. I tried to figure out what I'd do once I escaped. But my mind was too hazy from lack of food to think at all. The spilled gruel scene was repeated each day, along with Madame Bisset's fake, "Too bad." I feared I might soon consent to Madame Bisset's, "Would you like to return with me?" only out of starvation delirium. I thought I had been hungry before, but I'd never gone entirely without food.

On the third day, as soon as Madame Bisset was gone, I rushed to lick the floor where the gruel had fallen. I believe I managed to lap up only three flakes of meal and two weevils. But the sight of me on my knees sent Quog into howls of excitement.

"If you want me alive for the next two weeks," I said crossly, "you'll bring me more gruel."

Quog only howled louder.

Digging that night, I had to pause between each shovel load. I tried to remember if any of my father's books had contained information about how long someone could live without food. Surely it was many days. Surely Madame Bisset would not truly let me starve.

"Princess?"

With renewed energy, I scrambled out of the hole.

"Mary?"

"I brought you some food," she whispered. "I thought, with all that digging . . ."

Tears of relief blurred my eyes.

"You have saved my life," I blubbered. "I can't thank you enough. I can't—" I couldn't talk anymore, for cramming bread and cheese into my mouth.

"Don't they feed you?" Mary asked.

"No," I said.

She was silent, as if attempting to grasp their strategy.

"They think you'll cave soon," she said finally.

I didn't care about anything but the food in my mouth.

"Is there more?" I asked.

She laughed.

"Cook's off tonight. I can get lots. Have you dug enough of the hole that you can hide a big bundle?"

"Oh, yes!"

She brought what looked like a treasure trove of plums and pears and apples, an entire wheel of cheese, and three loaves of bread. I was crying with joy as she handed each food through my bars.

"Don't go on like that, please," she begged. "It's only plain stuff. I thought the fancy things might be missed."

"You don't understand. Weevils were starting to taste good to me. And then there's Quog—"

"Is he here?" Mary asked. Her voice trembled.

"Yes," I said. "He's my jailer. Lovely gentleman, isn't he?"

"Then you should dig fast."

I couldn't get her to explain more.

"I don't want to scare you," she said.

"But you already have," I muttered.

"Sorry," she said. "I should go. I'll try to come back the next time cook's off."

I started to protest, wanting company now that my belly would let me think of something besides food. But her words "You should dig fast" were still echoing in my ears. I went back into the crap hole and dug as much as I'd dug the previous two nights put together.

23

By the end of the fifth night, I was ready to curve my tunnel upward. I estimated it would take me only an hour or two from there, because I'd be helped by gravity bringing the dirt down. Would I dare break through the surface and escape at five in the morning?

Reluctantly, I decided it was too much risk. I wanted to put an entire night's travel between me and the castle before my disappearance was discovered. I put my shovel down and crawled back to my cell.

That next day was an agony. To be so close to freedom, but not to have it, made Quog's disgusting leers and taunts even more unendurable. When Madame Bisset showed up for the noon gruel routine, I had to struggle not to laugh in her face. *You've had five days of torture,* I told myself. *You can't act like you have any hope.*

"Have you come to your senses yet?" she asked.

"I still have senses about me," I retorted. "But—can't you feed me?"

Immediately, I realized my voice was too strong and self-assured.

"Please?" I made myself whimper. "I'm starving."

I sucked in my cheeks, although I thought the cell was too dark for her to notice that I wasn't as emaciated as I should be after five days without food.

Madame Bisset looked puzzled.

"Quog hasn't been bringing you extra food, has he?" she asked, her eyes narrowed.

I pretended to misunderstand.

"Oh, would he do that? That would be so wonderful. It doesn't have to be much—just a crust of bread. I won't get too fat, I promise. But I have to eat something. Oh, all I think about is food—"

"Here's your gruel, then," Madame Bisset said.

This time Madame Bisset herself passed the bowl through the bars. I made myself grab at it clumsily, feigning an eagerness only a starving person could have for that lukewarm, weevil-studded mess. My acting was too effective: This time I was the one who spilled it all over the floor.

I immediately fell to my knees and pretended to lick it up, right there in front of Madame Bisset.

"Mmm, mmm." I faked ecstasy at the taste of food. "Isn't there more? Please?"

"You are disgusting," Madame Bisset snapped.

But she finally sounded satisfied.

Two hours later I discovered my pretense had worked too well. The prince showed up.

"Oh, Ella," he declared with what was probably supposed to be a horrified tone, but only came out sounding wooden. "Is this where you've been? I didn't know— Oh, my beloved—"

I decided the supposed Prince of Charm was in desperate need of acting classes. But how in the world was I supposed to respond?

"Prince?" I said tentatively, buying time.

"It's those advisers of mine," he said. I think he may have been reading his words off a slip of paper in his hand. "They were angry at you. But I couldn't think of anything but you. I've searched the whole castle for you. I love you. I've missed you."

I stifled the urge to tell him I'd seen children display more genuine emotion over pet fleas they killed five minutes later. It probably wasn't in my best interest to speak of killing.

"You know, you are the prince. All you had to do was threaten to get rid of your advisers if they wouldn't tell you where I was," I said, flirting with insubordination in spite of myself.

The prince blinked. I don't think that line was in his script.

"I've come to rescue you," he said uncertainly.

Oh no! I couldn't leave the dungeon now!

"Come with me," the prince added. He raised a key to my door.

Thinking fast, I threw myself at the prince's feet—or as near as I could, with the dungeon door between us.

"But Sire," I wailed. "I wronged you. I deserve to stay here an entire week, to do penance for my sin."

I think "penance" was too complicated a word for the prince—after all, it does have two syllables. He stood there looking confused.

"Return for me in two days," I begged him. "Then I can go with you a pure woman, worthy of your love." I practically choked on the words. But, hey, my acting was no more appalling than the prince's.

"Well . . . ," the prince started doubtfully.

Down the hall I heard a growl.

"Who there?" Quog bellowed. "She mine!"

In the flickers of the lamplight, I saw the prince draw his sword.

"Begone!" he warned.

Quog stamped closer.

"Mine!" he repeated.

The prince ran his sword through Quog's chest.

"Argh!" Quog groaned. He fell heavily to the ground. Then he was silent.

The prince looked back at me, blood on his hands.

"I slew that creature for love of you," he mumbled.

I shrank back against the wall of my cell, weeping. I had no affection for Quog, of course, but what I had witnessed still horrified me. It was all so cold and heartless and without reason. Did the prince—or, more likely, his advisers—think I would be won over by watching him murder Quog? Did they understand me so poorly? What kind of people had I been living with?

"Darling," the prince said.

I sobbed harder.

"Now . . ." I could barely speak. "Now . . . I . . . am . . . truly . . . unworthy. Return in . . . three days."

"Oh, all right," the prince said, seeming suddenly impatient with the whole charade. "Bye."

He turned to go, kicking Quog's body aside without a second glance. I watched the circle of his lamplight recede down the hall with him. Even that dim glow picked up the glints of gold in his hair. I now knew the real Prince Charming to be, at best, an insensitive dullard, or perhaps even a callous monster only barely better than Quog himself. But I still felt a pang for the ideal I'd thought I'd loved, the perfect male I'd made up in my mind with the image of the prince's face.

I lay down on my plank bed and tried to forget what I'd seen. In three hours I would begin to dig. And then I could leave everything behind.

24

I dozed fitfully, only deep enough in sleep to dream. I saw Quog and the prince's bloody hands again and again. I think I cried out once or twice, but no one came to comfort me. I dreamed that Quog rose again and came and stood over my bed. Then Quog became the prince, reaching for me. I turned to him, forgetting my revulsion, forgetting everything but that beautiful face and handsome body. But as soon as I touched his hand, he turned into Quog.

I screamed myself awake.

Shaking, I sat up and wondered if I dared scramble over to the tunnel and make my escape. I wasn't concerned about anyone coming to investigate my screams. But what if someone came back for Quog's body? I made myself tiptoe over to the door and peek out. Staring into the darkness, I tried to make out a lump on the floor where Quog had fallen, or a trail of blood, but I couldn't make out anything, either way.

I went back and looked up at the window,

trying to evaluate how late it was. I was squinting into more darkness when I heard a blessed sound: the donging of the palace clock. Trembling, I counted carefully, as if everything depended on my accuracy. One, two, three . . . ten, eleven, twelve. I laughed, almost giddy.

It was time.

With a practiced air, I slid down the crap hole for the last time and shimmied into my tunnel. Preferring speed over style, I'd made it barely wide enough, so I had to perform a complicated dance maneuvering around the shovel and the bag of food Mary had brought me. The bag had grown light over the past two days, and I wished I could wait and restock it. I also hated the thought of leaving without saying good-bye and thanking Mary. But nothing could make me stay a minute longer in the castle than I had to.

Frantic with anticipation, I thrust my shovel again and again into the roof of my tunnel, not pausing even to brush away the clods of dirt that rained down on me. I got dirt in my eyes and kept shoveling. I got a splinter in my hand and ignored it. Then finally I felt something different brush my face with the falling soil. Something soft.

Grass.

Without thinking I jumped up, my head bursting through what remained of my tunnel's ceiling. The cool night air felt like a caress against my face. I had to stifle a shriek of glee.

I was out.

Caution overtook me after a second; I crouched and looked carefully around. There were lanterns at intervals along the castle wall behind me, but I saw no guards. I reached back into my tunnel and grabbed my food bag. When I noticed the shovel—my best friend for five days, now nearly forgotten—I picked it up to take along too, just in case it could incriminate Mary. I liked the notion of leaving people wondering how I'd gotten out. Let them think I'd dug through the crap hole with my fingernails. I grinned, remembering how the prim ladies-in-waiting always reacted in horror if anyone broke a fingernail during needlepoint. I wanted my hands to be more useful than that. I wanted my life to be more useful than that.

But just what was I going to do with it now?

25

If I'd been Jed, I probably could have stood there by my tunnel for hours pondering the point of my life. But I didn't have that luxury. I was out of the dungeon, but certainly not out of danger. Trying to stay in darkness as much as possible, I crept along the castle wall to the boulevard that faced it. But the boulevard was wide and open and lit by ever-burning torches. I found an alley instead.

As I inched my way through the shadows—stepping on a cat's tail once, knocking over garbage pails twice—I tried to formulate a plan. The first thing I had to do was get rid of my dress. Though a bit soiled by a week in the dungeon, it was still clearly a royal thing, made with shimmery gold thread and fitted as no common clothes were. Anyone who saw me in it would notice. But a girl running around naked would stand out even more.

I prayed for the sight of a clothesline, with even a peasant tunic hanging on it. But then I stepped in a puddle up to my ankles, bringing back an awareness of weather that I'd totally forgotten in the castle. Puddles meant it had rained, which meant no self-respecting peasant would have laundry hanging out.

And anyhow, I would have felt bad about stealing something that may have been some poor woman's only belonging. It wasn't like I could have left her my dress in trade.

I had to go to Lucille's.

Even as I adjusted my course—turning down one alley after another, trying to head for the edge of the city that surrounded the castle—I marveled that I was thinking of the house I'd grown up in as Lucille's now, not as mine. I'd lived in the castle only two months. Was that all it took for me to relinquish my home? Of course, I'd left without a backward glance when the prince was at my side and I thought he was the man of my dreams. But now . . . I considered my emotions the way someone with a pulled tooth might explore the hole with his tongue. It was true. My fervor was gone. Home wasn't home anymore.

I slipped into the countryside beyond the city, and reflected that it was good I wasn't longing for home anymore. My old house would be the least safe place for me to stay. Once morning came and they started looking for me, I'd never be able to go home again.

This thought did cause me a pang, but I only walked faster. I was following the same path I'd taken the night of the ball, but that had been in early spring, and now it was the height of summer. The leaves that were only beginning to bud then were now full-fledged and luxurious. As

I ducked under a low branch, one leaf came off against my shoulder. Whimsically I picked it up, planning to tuck it into my bag as a memento. But it was dry and prematurely dead. Shivering, I dropped it. I took it as a sign, almost. What if my life were abbreviated like that leaf's? Surely my time in the castle wouldn't be all the spring and summer I ever got.

I reached the outskirts of my old village, trying not to remember how carefree and happy I'd felt leaving it two months earlier. A confused cock crowed as I entered the main square, and I hid behind a barrel by the store. But nobody stirred, and after a moment, I continued on my way.

Even in the moonlight, my old house looked untended. The garden in the front was overgrown with weeds, and a few shingles had fallen from the roof. I laughed to myself as I eased the gate open. So, Lucille couldn't take care of it without me. I wondered if she would ever put Corimunde and Griselda to work on it, or if she'd have to break down and hire help.

I went around to the back, for fear of being spotted from the street. I picked the lock on the door with a hairpin, feeling grateful that I'd learned how to do that one hot summer day when I was eight and bored.

The door creaked a bit upon opening, but I didn't worry. Corimunde and Griselda were sound sleepers, and Lucille's room was far away, at the front of the house. I tiptoed up the back stairs and into Corimunde's room. I heard her soft snore and was reassured as I searched through her wardrobe. She was slightly less huge than Griselda, and therefore the better one to take a dress from. In the dark I chose at random, and hoped I'd picked nothing that displayed Corimunde's penchant for fabrics with gargantuan, splashy flowers.

Back in her doorway, the garment clutched in my hand, I hesitated. I thought of going up to the attic and retrieving my mother's wedding dress, just for sentiment's sake. But for me, that dress would always be connected with the night of the ball, and that was no longer a pleasant memory. Instead, I turned down the hall to my father's old study. After he died, Lucille had ordered me again and again to remove and box up the hundreds of books that lined the walls, and again and again I had refused. That was one battle I had won. I couldn't entirely prevent Lucille from disposing of my father's most treasured possessions, but I certainly wasn't going to help.

I didn't dare light a lamp in the study, but there was enough moonlight to show that the bookshelves were still full. Thank goodness for Lucille's laziness. I ran my fingers along the spines of the books, almost weeping with relief. I grabbed a book at random and hugged it to my chest. How I'd missed books at the castle.

I resisted the urge to start sweeping books into my bag—I had to be selective. I picked ten books, then narrowed the choice to six. Books were heavy, and I was going to have a long way to walk, if I acted upon the idea that had begun flitting around my brain.

Three of the books I chose were entirely pragmatic: an

atlas, a physician's textbook, and a volume on plant and animal husbandry. Two were entirely frivolous: a collection of poems I had practically memorized anyway, and a book of stories my father had read to me before I learned to read to myself. The sixth book was philosophy.

With these volumes snugly packed in my bag, I looked around one last time, then crept out of the room and down the stairs. I stopped once more in the pantry and took as much food as I could carry. They owed me, I reminded myself. And pickings might be slim where I was going.

In the dark of the pantry I also slipped my royal gown off and pulled Corimunde's dress over my shoulders. It was enormous; I had to rip a swath off the bottom to belt it around my waist. I could alter it later. I went into the parlor and dug a needle and thread out of a sewing basket that probably hadn't been touched since I'd left with the prince.

Shoving my old gown into my already bulging pack, I considered leaving a note for Lucille and the Step-Evils, to warn them that the royal idiots would be looking for me. But they'd find out soon enough. I didn't owe Lucille any explanations. And it wasn't like the Step-Evils would be in danger. Even at their cruelest, I didn't think the so-called Charmings would punish Lucille for my desertion. No, I decided, I shouldn't take the time.

I shouldered my pack and stepped out the back door, pulling it shut behind me. But the latch jammed, probably because of my picking the lock. I didn't feel particularly guilty about that, and I could easily have walked away. But something made me want to shut the door good and tight on Lucille and the Step-Evils. I let my pack slide to the ground and swung the door open again, to jimmy the knob from the inside.

That's when I heard the footsteps.

"So," Lucille jeered. "The *princess* has returned."

26

I whirled around in a panic.

"You never wake up at night," I protested.

Lucille smirked.

"So how many nights did you spend sneaking out to visit paramours? I was right—you never were anything but a piece of gutter trash. And now that prince has used you and cast you aside, just as I predicted. At least my *real* daughters listen to their mother."

"I ran away," I said. "I—"

Lucille looked me up and down, her glittering eyes taking in the dirt on my face and in my hair. I held my breath, fearing she'd comment upon Corimunde's dress, but evidently it was too dark for her to notice. And she was too caught up in her mockery of my morals.

"Even you're not a big enough fool to run away from a prince," she sneered. "You'll have to come up with a cleverer story than that. But it matters not. Everyone will know what happened. You'll be the talk of the village tomorrow." She sighed, with a pretense of compassion. "Well, only a saint would take you back, under these circumstances, but I have been looking for a servant. . . . You may begin by fetching me my stomach elixir. That's what I came down here for in the first place. Something at supper didn't agree with me."

My jaw dropped. She wasn't even curious. I almost felt sorry for her. Her life was so small. If I told her everything, she wouldn't be able to grasp it.

"And then," Lucille continued, "you may scrub the kitchen floor. I want it clean by morning."

"I am not your servant. I will never be your servant again. I hope you and Corimunde and Griselda die in your own filth," I said.

And then I turned and ran, stooping to grab my bag as I zoomed by.

"Stop! Wait! Is that something of mine you're taking? Thief! Help, thief!"

I ran faster, the bag thumping against my back. Lucille made no attempt to follow me—I knew she wouldn't—but she screamed louder. "Stop! Thief! Help! Runaway servant!" I prayed that the neighbors were all sleeping soundly or, at least, wouldn't feel like rousing themselves for Lucille. That was a fairly safe bet.

I crashed through the back gate and into the woods beyond. I stepped into the creek that ran through our village and listened, my heart pounding. Lucille's shouts were distant now, and there were no answering bellows. I heard mostly crickets.

Trembling, I pulled my royal gown from my bag and let

it slide into the water. It caught on a rock, but then slithered forward, shimmering gold in the moonlight. The color reminded me of Prince Charming's hair. I tried not to think about how happy I'd expected to be, ever after, with everything shining around me. I watched the dress until it floated out of sight.

"Go far north," I whispered. "Cover for me." It suddenly struck me that north was the way to Domulia, the country the palace officials pretended I was from. Maybe someone had actually believed the story and would look in that direction first. If they found the dress, it might buy me enough time to get where I was really going.

I turned and began walking south, toward the Sualan border.

27

That first night was the hardest. I knew I had to cover far more territory than they'd expect me to, and I'd already wasted half the night. At first I fretted, "Will Jed really take me in at the refugee camp?" But after a few miles, my mind shut off, and all I could do was concentrate on walking—convincing exhausted muscles they would survive another step. And another. And another . . .

I stepped out of the creek when it turned westward, four miles south of my village. After hours in the water, my feet were numb, but surely the water had covered my tracks. I worried about the muddy footprints I left along the creek and stopped to wash them out behind me. Then I skulked along fence rows and forests until I saw the first glow of dawn on the horizon. I was on the edge of another village then, much too close for my taste. I could hear cocks beginning to crow, horses neighing in their stalls. I circled wide, stumbling through wheat fields. All I wanted to do was lie down and sleep. Did I dare hide in the wheat? It wasn't harvesttime yet, and why else would anyone investigate the field? I looked behind me at the trail of bent wheat plants. Oops. I found a path where I could leave no tracks and ran along it.

Finally, just as the sun appeared, I came to a ramshackle barn that obviously had been abandoned years before. I shoved my way in, praying for soft hay. There was none, only a row of barrels. I rolled one over on its side and crawled into it, pulling my dress around my feet.

I fell asleep instantly and didn't wake until dusk.

I followed that pattern—traveling by night, sleeping by day—for so many days, I lost count. I slept in haystacks, corncribs, caves, and once, when no better option showed up, on a tree limb. That choice almost proved disastrous, because I started rolling off the limb whenever I nodded off. I didn't get much sleep that day, and was stumbly and stupid the following night. But mostly I slept well. My body didn't protest the reversal of day and night at all, probably because I'd been working by night in the dungeon, as well.

By the third night, I began waking long before dusk, which allowed me to work on the second part of my plan: studying the medical and agricultural books. In my mind I played over and over again the scene of me arriving at Jed's refugee camp. I wouldn't beg. I would state my case calmly and clearly: "It is a risk to you to have me here, but I can be very useful too. I can treat the wounded people; I can teach them how to grow more food. And nobody will recognize me now."

I was sure of that. I left burrs in my hair and dirt on my face, like camouflage. And Corimunde's dress—which did, indeed, sport roses the size of cabbages—quickly grew so ragged and dirty, the pattern was barely visible.

Nobody saw me. I saw nobody, except at a great distance, in the dark. And then I always hid or got off the path to avoid them. By day I sometimes heard voices. I always woke in a panic, fearing they belonged to the king's soldiers, come to find me. But each time I was wrong, and I fell back to sleep listening to children playing games, women gossiping as they picked elderberries, men boasting as they scythed hay. The voices made me feel lonelier still. I had been an outsider at the castle, I had been an outsider with the Step-Evils; even as a child, happy with my father, I had known we were different from all the other families. Would I ever find where I belonged?

Sometimes, walking through the night, I thought back on the choices I'd made and where they'd led me, and somehow I did not regret any of them. Promising to marry the prince had turned out to be a bad idea, but life in the castle had certainly been an experience. I'd met Mary, who was the truest friend I could ever hope for, and I'd met Jed, who . . .

I didn't let myself examine my feelings for Jed. All I could hope for was that he'd save my skin. Whenever I started thinking about him, I forced myself to concentrate on reviewing medical treatments. "How do you treat

snakebite?" I quizzed myself. "What's the best way to set a broken arm?"

But as the days passed, I longed to have someone to talk to about my life: past, present, and ever after. At first I thought of Mary, who always listened so devotedly, but listening wasn't all I wanted. I wanted advice. I wanted someone older and wiser. More and more, I wished that, before Lucille had caught me that night I escaped from the castle, I'd had the sense to go next door and talk to my former neighbor, Mrs. Branson, who in the midst of taking care of her brood had given me all the mothering I'd ever gotten. "What is love, anyway?" I wanted to ask. I'd obviously been wrong about what I felt for Prince Charming, since it had soured so soon. Would I recognize real love if I ever found it? Did I even want it? It seemed easier to go through life the way my father had between my mother's death and Lucille's arrival: devoted to knowledge, not emotion. (How do you treat snakebite? What's the best way to set a broken arm?) But didn't I want my life to be something more than easy?

You'd think, with all the time I had to ponder everything, I'd have come up with some answers. But all I accomplished was to walk by night, sleep by day, and learn medicine and agriculture.

And then came the day I heard soldiers.

28

At sunup that day, I had chosen a hiding place in a meadow along the road. I knew it wasn't the safest spot, but nothing else was available, and the grass was so tall, it didn't look like anyone ever scythed it. I'd just hoped no one picked that day for the first cutting.

Judging by the position of the sun, it was just after noon when I woke to the tramping of feet.

"Company, halt!" Dozens of feet pounded the ground at once. "Fall out!"

Their sounds weren't so organized after that. The soldiers seemed to be stomping all over the place. I froze as I heard some of them scrambling up the bank near me.

". . . thought they'd march us straight to Suala all this morning—"

"This probably is Suala now. We probably lost half the territory while we were away."

So these soldiers weren't looking for me. They were simply on their way to fight Suala. But why were they climbing toward me?

Pssss. I heard the sound of several bladders

being relieved at once. Oh. I was safe as long as I didn't get wet.

I hoped the soldiers would go back to the road when they were done, but they didn't. They flopped down on the ground nearby and began ordering people around.

"See, I told you there'd be peasants around here," one muttered. Then he shouted, "Peasant, bring us a feast."

"F-feast?" a trembling voice replied. "We have no feast, only common food, and not much of that. You soldiers have taken it all—"

"Feed us or else!"

I don't know what the soldier did—drew a sword? grabbed the peasant by the neck?—but the peasant immediately began stammering, "Yes, sir. Yes, sir."

The soldiers laughed.

In a short while, I began to smell the irresistible aroma of cooking meat. Since I'd been living on stale bread, hard cheese, and the odds and ends of fruit I could pick up along the way, my mouth began watering almost unbearably. It was torture to listen to the soldiers smacking their lips and chewing and belching. Finally, though, I heard one proclaim, "Aye, peasant, I knew that you could find a way to feed us. Fine vittles, I must say."

"Ought to be," the peasant mumbled. "That was all we had stored for the winter."

"Oh?" the solder said, as if he truly cared not. "Then I suppose we owe you something. How about a story?"

"A story?" Perhaps only I could tell how hard the peasant was trying not to sound scornful.

"Aye. We have been at the prince's wedding—"

It was a good thing I was already lying down, because that statement would have knocked me to the ground. What could he mean? I knew Prince Charming was the only prince around. How could he have found someone else so fast? I didn't love him, and was glad not to be marrying him, but still . . .

Evidently one of the peasant women was practically as stunned as I was.

"You haven't!" she declared. "Bunch of filthy fighting men like yourselves wouldn't be invited to any royal wedding."

"Were too!" the soldier countered. "We were the royal battalion. One of them, anyway. There were one hundred rows of us marching with the prince's carriage and another hundred with the princess's."

"Did you see the princess?" the woman asked wistfully. "Was she beautiful?"

I peeked through the grass and saw the woman asking the questions. She was old and toothless, her hair hidden in a kerchief, her shoulders stooped with years of hard labor. She couldn't have been waiting for the soldier's answer any more eagerly than I was.

"We were too far back," the soldier said. "And she had a veil over her face."

"There were those flowers too," another soldier reminded him.

"Yeah, they had these bunches of flowers all over the place, blocking our view."

Not to be deterred, the woman asked, "What kind of flowers?"

"How am I to know? I'm a soldier, not a gardener."

"Orchids," someone else contributed.

The first soldier wasn't done speaking.

"But I'll tell you, even if I didn't see her, I know that princess must be about the most beautiful woman ever. Did you hear the story about her? She was just this commoner living with her cruel stepmother and stepsisters after her father died. And then the prince gave a ball and the stepmother wouldn't let this girl go."

I got chills. I could hardly listen.

"Cinderella, everyone called her, because she had to sleep in the cinders and was filthy all the time—"

That's not true! I wanted to protest. Only Corimunde and Griselda called me that. And it was Cinders-Ella, anyway. And I took baths more often than either of them, so I was hardly filthy. . . . I pressed my lips together to make myself stay silent.

"So, after her stepmother and stepsisters left for the ball, Cinderella lay weeping in the ashes, and suddenly her fairy godmother appeared."

I lay numb for the rest of the story. I'd never heard all the details before, only whispered bits and pieces at the palace and the abbreviated tale Jed had told me. In its entirety, the story was even more ridiculous than I had supposed. Why in the world would I have had mice as friends? And if I already had a horse, why would my supposed fairy godmother bother turning the mice into horses? The absurdities went on and on.

The soldier finally ended, "And at the wedding, they pledged to love each other forever and live happily ever after."

"Ooh," the peasant woman sighed breathlessly. "I just love a good romance."

The soldier snorted. "You women," he said, but he had a softness to his voice, as if he liked the story too, even if he wouldn't admit it.

I gripped the grass with my hands, angry beyond words. These people had been tricked so badly. I didn't know who they'd found to stand in my place at the wedding—I didn't really care—but people should know there wasn't a fairy godmother involved in the true story. They should know the prince wasn't exactly charming after all, and nobody had an ant's chance in an elephant stampede of living happily ever after with him. Maybe it was possible for people to fall in love and marry and be happy together, but my story hardly proved the point.

So why were these lies being spread?

"For-ma-a-tion!" an official-sounding voice snapped from across the road.

The soldiers scurried into position, and in a few moments I heard them marching on again. I still lay tense and worried while the peasants cleaned up behind them, but soon they left too. I strained my ears, but could hear nothing but the buzz of insects and the whoosh of wind blowing through the grass.

I was safe again. I had not been discovered.

But I couldn't get back to sleep. After days of sleeping without problem on rocks, hay, roots, and assorted other discomforts, I was suddenly unable to settle down on the soft grass beneath me. The heat made my head ache, and I had the strange urge to cry.

I opened the medical book to study since I couldn't sleep, but the words only swam before my eyes.

Why did everyone like that story so much when it wasn't true? Why was everyone so eager to believe it? Was it because, in real life, ever after's generally stink?

Would mine?

29

In two nights' time, I was close enough to the Sualan border to hear the sounds of battle. I had read about plenty of wars in my father's books, but no book could have prepared me for the screams of anguish and terror I heard every day when I hid and tried to sleep. A thousand times over, I pictured the prince slaying Quog—the only killing I'd ever witnessed. I remembered my father dying while crossing the Sualan border, all because one side thought he might be a spy for the other. "It's not worth it," I whispered in my abandoned sheds and dusty haystacks. "This land is not worth dying for." I decided that Jed, for the first time in his life, had focused on too small an issue. He shouldn't be helping the refugees; he should be trying to end the war so there would be no refugees.

I reminded myself I had a more immediate problem than the Sualan War.

I still puzzled over the story the soldier had told to the peasants. Had the wedding really taken place without me? And if so, did that mean I was safe? Or, at least, safer?

I decided it did. The morning of the third day after I'd heard the soldiers—something like the fourteenth day after my escape from the palace—I allowed myself to be seen. I kept walking after daybreak, until I came to a man working in a field.

"Sir, please, could you tell me . . ." After two weeks of talking to no one but myself, my voice was rusty. "Could you tell me how to get to a place where they help people who have lost their homes in the war?"

He looked up slowly, his rheumy eyes heavy with a look I couldn't understand at first.

"Ye lost your home, now," he started.

He thought I was one of the refugees. He pitied me.

I rushed to explain.

"No, no, I'm not, that is—" I looked down at Corimunde's dress, hanging loosely on my frame. Some-how I'd never bothered altering it. That hardly mattered now. After all my nights of traveling, the dress was filthy and ragged beyond repair. I touched my hair—filled with brambles and dirt. I touched my face—streaked with mud and sweat. No wonder he took me for a war refugee. I looked like one.

I felt ashamed of appearing so needy. But I decided not to correct his error. I had lost my home, after all, just not because of the war.

"That place you're talking about," the man said. "It's up the road a ways. Turn left at the crooked tree. You'll see it. People have worn a path there." He hesitated. "I don't usually do this, because I can't be feeding every Tom, Dick, and Harry that comes along. But do ye need any food before ye go?"

I didn't realize I looked that bad.

"No, thank you," I said, trying to sound dignified.

His "a ways" turned out to be an entire morning's walk. Again and again, I fretted that I'd missed the crooked tree—not exactly the easiest landmark to find. I puzzled over several slightly gnarled elms and one twisted pine. When I finally came to the apple tree growing at an almost forty-five-degree angle to the ground, I noticed the path beside it before I noticed the tree. The path was wide and beaten down, its dirt packed as firmly as that of the road I was on.

Jed evidently had had lots of visitors.

I turned down the path and walked perhaps half a mile before a long, low building appeared over the next rise. Knots began to tie in my stomach. If Jed didn't let me stay, where else could I go?

I looked down at my dress again, and wished I could find a creek to wash in. But I was too close now to put up with any delays, and there wasn't a creek in sight.

And I had to make sure no one would recognize me as the missing princess—if anybody here knew I was missing.

I reached the gate by the building in no time. It held no sign announcing the camp's purpose, but I could see dozens of people inside the gate. A row of men were cutting silage, while others stood around tanning animal skins, chopping firewood, or, at the very least, whittling.

At the other end of the yard, women were kneading bread, sewing clothes, or stirring boiling vats of what smelled like lye soap. It seemed a very busy, happy place, except that when people raised their heads to look at me, I saw vacant eyes and faces etched with sorrow. These people hadn't just heard the war. They had seen it.

"Excuse me," I said to one of the women. "I'm looking for Jed Reston."

Silently, she pointed toward the main building.

I stepped in to see rows of beds, like a dormitory. This evidently was the children's domain during the day. Some played hide-and-seek among the bedding, but others were just sitting still, staring into space.

"I'm trying to find Jed Reston," I said to a girl about my age, who looked to be baby-sitting.

"Office is over there," she said with the kind of insolent shrug I'd used so often on Lucille.

I knocked at the office door. A woman's voice called a cheery, "Come in!"

"I need to see Jed Reston," I repeated once again when I'd entered and found only a plump, middle-aged woman seated at the desk before me.

"Oh, no, you don't," she replied, still cheerful. "You just check in with me, that's all you have to do. We'll get you set right up."

So I was mistaken for a refugee once again. For a split second I considered going along with the charade. I could probably manage to keep Jed from ever seeing me. I pictured my future, sent out to some patch of farmland safely away from the war, safely away from the castle and Lucille. I could have my own hut, raise my own food. It might not be bad.

But I did want to see Jed. I wanted to tell him everything that had happened, ask him his opinions, find out how his dream was turning out. I couldn't come this far and hide from him.

"You don't understand," I told the too-cheerful woman. "I'm not a refugee. I'm an old friend of Jed's. Could someone tell him that, um . . . Ella is here?"

I just hoped Jed would recognize my nonroyal name.

The woman narrowed her eyes, not missing my hesitation. I think she took me for some unsavory companion from his past, one he was better off rid of. And perhaps that was true, though not for the reasons the woman imagined. If the prince found out I was here, it wouldn't be good for Jed.

"And will he want to see you?" she asked.

"I think so," I said. "Yes."

The door behind me pushed open.

I turned around to see the intruder, and it was Jed. He stopped short at the sight of me.

"Ella," he breathed in a voice that made my heart beat fast and my head feel light. I didn't realize Jed could have that effect on me. But I was so exhausted and hungry, my body's reactions weren't very reliable.

I tried to recall what I'd planned to say, to convince him to let me stay.

"I ran away," I started. "I—" I remembered the woman

at the desk. I turned around and saw she was leaning forward, listening intently.

"Mrs. Smeal, could you go check on the bedding supply?" Jed asked.

"I just counted all the blankets yesterday," she replied.

"Count them again," Jed ordered. He had a tone in his voice I'd never heard back at the castle. He seemed more confident, older.

"But—" Mrs. Smeal still protested.

Jed gave her a look that silenced her immediately. She slunk out the door with an injured air.

Jed took my hands in his.

"Are you all right?" he asked. "You look—"

"A little worse for wear?" I finished his sentence ruefully. "Digging out from a dungeon will do that to a girl. So will walking for two weeks."

Jed looked confused.

"But a rider came out and told us about the wedding only yesterday. He said it took place last Friday."

"There may have been a wedding," I retorted, "but I wasn't there."

I told him my story. I think I must have gotten some of it a little garbled, because he stopped me after a few moments, put his arm around me, and led me to a couch. Then he put his head out the door and called, "Ermaline, can you bring me a bowl of that stew left over from lunch?"

I ate like a starving person, which I basically was. Then I continued my tale. Jed interrupted only once more.

"They had Quog guarding you?" he protested when I reached that part. "But he was sentenced to death weeks ago."

"What for?" I asked.

"Rape." Jed looked away. "Many of them."

I took a shaky breath.

"I guess he got a stay of execution, until the prince could deliver the sentence personally. Oh, Jed, Quog was just a prop to them, something to scare me into submission. And then they actually thought I'd leap into the prince's arms with joy, seeing him slaughter Quog—"

"They didn't know you very well," Jed murmured.

Even with the stew making me feel steadier, I couldn't quite read Jed's expression. I hurried through the rest of the story and finished up, ". . . so you can see there aren't very many places in the kingdom that I'd be welcome. And I know I might be endangering you and your cause by coming here. But I did study those books, and I know I would be useful."

"Oh, Ella," Jed hugged me tight. "You should have known I would never turn you away. But I have a better plan."

He slid down and crouched on the floor before me. Awkwardly, he put first his right knee on the ground, then his left. Then he raised his right knee again and leaned toward me. I couldn't figure out what he was doing. He took my hands in his once more.

"Ella," he said solemnly, "will you marry me?"

30

I jerked my hands back in shock.

"What?" I asked.

Jed looked sheepish, but persevered.

"I want you to marry me," he repeated.

"I don't need that kind of charity," I said sulkily. Who would ever have thought: For all that I'd always said I didn't care about marriage, I kept getting the most unexpected offers.

Jed raised his earnest face toward mine. To my surprise, he had tears sparkling in his eyes.

"It's not charity," he said. "Don't you know? I've been in love with you since that first day I met you. From the moment you opened that door, when I came to tutor you."

I remembered the thunderstruck look on his face.

"No offense," I said. "But I'm not too impressed with the concept of love at first sight right now. You heard where it got me. Anyhow, I don't exactly look the way I did then. So you can forget that sight."

Jed reached up and touched my face. I didn't

move away. I was trying to decide if I liked it.

"You still look beautiful to me," he said softly. "But it's not your looks I'm in love with. Or," he corrected himself, "not just them. It's your personality, and your sense of humor, your courage, your perseverance, your intelligence. . . . Basically, everything about you."

"You sure had a funny way of showing your love," I grumbled. "Why didn't you tell me before?"

"You were betrothed to the prince," he said. "I thought you loved him."

"I thought so too," I admitted. "But you knew he was a jerk and a fool. Why didn't you tell me?"

Jed only looked at me. I thought about how it would sound if he'd told me any time at the palace, "I love you. And, oh, by the way, that guy you're engaged to is a lout."

"Okay," I said. "I guess that wouldn't have worked." I thought about the awkward silences that had developed between me and Jed, the questions he'd avoided answering, the moments I'd wondered how he could suddenly seem as distant as the prince himself. "It must have been torture for you."

Jed nodded silently. A moment passed before he admitted softly, "I couldn't stand to call you 'Princess' or hear anyone else refer to you as 'Princess,' because that reminded me you would never be mine. So in my mind you were always just 'Ella' when I thought about you, which was about twenty-seven hours a day. Sometimes, when we were together, and I wanted so badly to give up the pretense and pull you into my arms and—well, you know—I'd make myself call you 'Princess' to hold myself back."

"I remember," I said softly.

"And when I was given permission to build the camp, all I wanted to do was come and tell you, but I knew if I did, I'd forget myself and throw myself at your feet and beg you to come along. So I didn't even say good-bye—"

"I noticed," I said drily. "You would have had trouble finding me in the dungeon."

"I'm sorry," Jed said. "I didn't know. Obviously. . ."

He shook his head, as if trying to shake off the past.

"But that's over, and we're together now." His eyes shone with hope, waiting for my reply. Then he winced, and I realized he'd been crouching on the floor for an awfully long time.

"Why don't you get up?" I asked. "I think you only have to make the proposal on bended knee. You can be comfortable to hear the answer."

"Oh. Okay." Jed sounded relieved as he got up and sat beside me. He started to reach for my hand again but stopped himself. "And the answer is?"

His hands were suspended, midreach. I thought about it. I had to believe he really did love me. Did I love him? I didn't feel for him the way I'd felt for the prince, back when I thought I loved him. But I knew now that that had been infatuation with an ideal, not love for a real human being. Jed was real. I knew his faults as well as his virtues and didn't mind them. I enjoyed being with him. I'd certainly rushed to find him as soon as I could. Of all the men I'd ever met, he was the one I'd want to marry the most. But I was only fifteen. I hadn't really met that many men. And, beyond that, I hadn't really figured out what I wanted to do with my life. Marriage could determine what was possible or impossible. What if, after a few years, Jed and I turned out to have goals as mismatched as my father's and Lucille's?

I looked away, because I couldn't bear to watch Jed's face when he heard what I had to say.

"The answer is, I don't know. Or—" I made the mistake of turning toward him. I caught a glimpse of his crestfallen face. I looked down at my hands, still alone in my lap. Jed had drawn back. I made myself look directly at him. "The best thing I can say is, I can't make any promises yet. I thought I loved the prince, and I thought I was doing the right thing agreeing to marry him. So how good can my judgment be?"

"But you learned from that," Jed protested. "You know me better than you knew him."

"True. But when I agreed to marry him, I was thinking mainly of getting away from—and getting back at—Lucille. Now I'm trying to escape the prince. If I were to marry you, wouldn't you rather it be because I'm trying to get *to* you, instead of *away* from someone else?"

"Why can't it be both?" Jed joked.

I only shook my head, then added, "Can't you give me six months and ask again?"

There was a tap at the door before the formerly cheerful Mrs. Smeal poked her head in. "I know this will amaze you, Chief, but we still have 402 blankets stacked up in the supply tent. Same as yesterday."

Jed blinked.

"Oh," he said. "I thought we had a new shipment in. Wasn't there a royal proclamation to that effect?"

I barely listened to Mrs. Smeal's answer. I had to figure out where I would go and what I would do now. Under the circumstances, it seemed too much to expect Jed to let me hang out at the camp. Then I heard him say, "Mrs. Smeal, may I introduce Ella Brown, our new medical and agricultural adviser?"

Mrs. Smeal's jaw dropped, and her eyes seemed to come very close to jumping out of their sockets. But she was polite enough to say only, "Welcome. We're glad to have you."

I looked at Jed, instead of her, as I replied, "Thank you."

31

As the next few months passed, I splinted an amazing number of broken arms. I treated everything from bee stings to gores from a wild boar. I ladled out gallons of soup in the camp's kitchen. One incredible rainy night in a far pasture, I delivered a calf that was trying to be born hind end first. I worked harder than I'd ever worked for Lucille.

And every evening I spent hours talking to Jed.

At first we were awkward together. What hadn't been decided stood like an uninvited guest between us. But then we agreed not to speak of love or marriage or the future until the six months were up. Those subjects still crept into our conversations occasionally. Jed would say, "When we're running the camp as partners . . . er, I mean—" and, "When we have children—that is, uh. . . ." Or I'd say, "What if I decide I want to go learn more about being a doctor? Could I do that and be married?" Jed would assure me, "We can work it out." But because we weren't going to make any decisions for six months, most of the time we just talked and talked, as good friends do. Jed treasured the philosophy book I'd brought him, and we took turns puzzling out its meaning. Sometimes, when we were both too exhausted to think, I read stories to him out loud. We debated good and evil, argued about how the Sualan War could end.

I was, strangely enough, happy.

Then one day, while I was checking on patients in the makeshift infirmary, a girl summoned me to the office.

"Can't it wait?" I asked. I was trying to decide if the feverish baby lying listlessly on the table in front of me had a disease that could spread through the whole camp.

"No," the girl said. "Master Reston said now."

I turned. Except for the war-haunted eyes, the girl reminded me of Mary.

"All right," I said. "He'll be fine," I told the baby's mother, with a confidence I didn't feel. "But keep him away from the other children."

She stared at me hopelessly. How to keep a baby away from other children when their entire family was sleeping in one bed?

I worried about that as I walked back to the office. But I forgot my worries when I arrived and Jed wordlessly thrust a card into my hand. It was thick and luxurious, its words in such fancy script that it took me a few minutes to read them:

*We regret to inform you of the death of His Excellency,
the Lord Maximilian Reston. Please return to the castle
immediately to take over his duties.*

*By proclamation of
King Charming XXIII*

"Oh, Jed, I'm sorry," I said, echoing the useless words
that Jed had said to me all those months ago when I'd told
him of my father's death.

"Why?" Jed said in a choked voice. "Why does it hurt
so much? I didn't even like him."

"But he was your father," I said.

"Couldn't they have broken the news in a nicer way?"
Jed asked plaintively. "The king could have offered his
condolences or something."

I thought of Lucille sneering at me, "Your father's dead.
Get to work." Essentially, that was the king's message too,
only in fancier language. I felt grateful once again that I
was away from the so-called Charmings. But I still felt bad
for Jed. He didn't even seem to have absorbed the second
half of the message.

"It doesn't matter how anyone says it," I said gently. "It
still hurts."

"When does it stop hurting?" he asked.

"I don't know," I said. "It takes longer than three years."

And then I hugged him, and he hugged me, and it
wasn't the least bit romantic—not like dancing under the
stars on a rose-scented night—but it was still the most

romantic moment of my life. He pulled back first.

"I want you to run the camp while I'm away," he said. So he had read the whole note.

"Why me?" I asked. "Why not Mrs. Smeal? Why not one of the men?"

"You know," Jed said. And I did—Mrs. Smeal was too cheerful, unable to understand true problems. The refugees made fun of her behind her back. And the two male workers at the camp had only contempt for the refugees, as though it were their fault for being displaced by the war. So I might be the best choice. But could I do it? Did I want to?

"You'll have to let them think they have some control," Jed continued. "They don't know how young you really are, but still—"

I nodded knowingly. I'd learned a lot more diplomacy at the camp than at the castle.

"For how long?" I asked. "Are you—are you coming back?" Something crept into my voice—a hint that I wanted him back for more than the smooth running of the camp.

"Absolutely," he said firmly. "If nothing else, I'll write you for escape tips."

And so he rode away, and I missed him, and I waited for him to come back. I remembered what one of my attendants back at the castle had said the day of the tournament: "This is what women do. We wait." I'd vowed to have none of that. But here I was, waiting.

Only I wasn't sitting around doing pointless needle-point. I was binding wounds, ordering supplies, standing up to bitter refugees who questioned why a mere girl should be able to tell them how much firewood they were allowed to have. I fell into bed many nights too exhausted to think. Every once in a while, a strange thought drifted into my head: *If I have no life's goal of my own, is it such a bad thing to do the life's work of the man I love?*

I didn't quite allow myself to think the word *love.* I thought *respect, care about.*

After a month, a letter arrived from Jed. Though it was the middle of the day, and I had about ten days' worth of work to do in the next hour, I immediately shut the door of the office and sat down to read.

> *Dear Ella,*
>
> *The castle remains mostly as you remember it: dull, dreary, obsessed with the most ridiculous minutiae. I promise I won't get mushy, but I long to be back at the camp with you. How many people are coming per day? How many have you resettled? Are supplies getting through? If you need to— (Here he scratched out something.)*
>
> *I'm sorry—I'm sure you're handling everything fine.*
>
> *I have news that will amuse—or bemuse—or at least interest—you. I have found the answer to the mystery about who they found to replace you at the prince's wedding. Are you sitting down? It's your sister—stepsister— Corimunde.*

I dropped the letter in astonishment. After I picked it
up, I rubbed my eyes for several minutes hoping to get
them to read properly. But when I looked at the letter
again, it still distinctly said "Corimunde." I read on.

> *It was Madame Bisset's idea—a stroke of genius in*
> *many respects, I might add. It certainly saved her skin.*
> *And yours. I've learned the whole story, mainly by*
> *appearing absolutely disinterested. Madame Bisset evi-*
> *dently argued that since you were obviously unre-*
> *deemable (her words, not mine), they should not bother*
> *chasing you. You'd only make more trouble as a wife*
> *and, eventually, as a mother. Instead, she said, they*
> *should go back to the original source. I thought that*
> *would have been an argument for another ball and*
> *beauty contest, etc., etc., but the royal advisers all*
> *thought that might be too embarrassing. They argued,*
> *would anyone want to be the prince's betrothed when the*
> *last one had mysteriously disappeared—maybe died?*
> *Figuring that only your family would have as much rea-*
> *son as the Charmings to want to keep everything secret,*
> *the king's herald went back to your house and swept*
> *away the first girl who answered the door.*

Corimunde always had been a little quicker on her feet
than Griselda.

> *You'll be amused to know that the style now among*
> *castle women is, the fatter the better. Another of*

Madame Bisset's ideas, I believe. My conjecture is that she took one look at Corimunde and decided it would be easier to change the fashion than your sister. After she failed so dramatically trying to change you, Madame Bisset seems a little worn out and more likely to go for the easy solution.

So had I actually changed Madame Bisset, instead of the other way around? Was she even becoming flexible? But no—I read on—it sounded like this beauty standard was being enforced as rigidly as the last one.

You wouldn't recognize many of your ladies-in-waiting anymore, they've gained so much weight. I don't think there's a corset left among them. Cyronna and Simprianna eat nonstop, though they have quite a ways to go before they'll be as "beautiful" as Corimunde. Really, you exaggerated somewhat about her appearance. She's not that bad-looking if you squint a little. She's brought Griselda and your stepmother into the castle as well. They appear quite happy and, I must say, Corimunde and the prince do seem suited to each other. I believe she is with child, though no announcement has been made yet.

I leaned back to absorb this incredible news. I could imagine Lucille gloating at the thought of being with her "real" daughters in the castle while I was who knows where—on the streets, perhaps even dead. I furrowed my brow, trying to figure out what I felt. Was I jealous? I remembered my last taunt to Lucille: "I hope you and Corimunde and Griselda die in your own filth!" But I had been angry then. I no longer wished them ill. I certainly had no desire to be in the castle, and if Corimunde and the prince were well suited, more power to them. It was just that, by Lucille's terms, she had won and I had lost.

Only I had no desire to judge myself by Lucille's terms anymore.

I skipped ahead, more curious about what Jed was doing than about the Step-Evils.

> *I am personally handling all the supply requests for the camp, because no one else cares. They think that now I'm back, the camp has been disbanded. I don't necessarily correct them, though I'd like to. You were right that they allowed me to set up the camp in the first place only because they wanted me out of the castle. I think Madame Bisset, at least, guessed that I was (am) in love with you, and she knew I wouldn't stand for putting you in the dungeon. (I'm surprised they thought I had that much power.) Several people have tried to discover if I know where you are now, but, of course, I'm pretending not to. I did find Mary and thanked her for her help and told her that you're safe. She asked if we were "hitched" yet. (I'm not making this up!) I said I'd asked, but you wanted to wait. She said, and I quote, "Me mum says that's the surest way to lose a man." I told her, not this man. I also told her, if we do get married, our marriage*

won't be like other people's. You may go off and study to become a full-fledged doctor. We may work as a team on everything. Mary said, and I quote again, "Is that supposed to surprise me? You and the princess have never been like anybody else."

But your six-month deadline is only a month away, and I will probably still be here at the castle then. I could take an exit route similar to yours; I'm not as practiced at walking from the castle to the camp as you are, but I'm sure I could manage. If I played my cards right, I could probably make a more subtle retreat, working my younger brother into this position. I'm pretty sure I could convince the king that Joseph's a better adviser than I am. But I can't leave now, or even a month from now, because I think I can end the Sualan War. That is not more important than you, or us, but . . . oh, I think you understand. You were right in all our debates: Ending the war is a better goal than simply helping those hurt by the war. Few people here care either way—if anything, they like having the war around as an interesting topic of discussion. But I've been dropping hints about how much the royal treasury is being drained, how much wealth is being wasted. (As you know, they don't care about lives.) I think I've convinced the king he could build a more sumptuous palace with the fortune he'd save by ending the war. I've almost convinced him to let me lead a peace mission to Suala.

So. I think about you all the time, you there, me here. I miss you. I long to come and get you and run

away together somewhere and forget this stupid king-
dom. But I can't. I can't do that and be worthy of you. I
think about how you were brave enough to take your
fate into your own hands—not once, but twice. You
inspire me. So will you now wait for me?

With all my love,
Jed

I lowered the letter slowly, feeling torn. So Jed might
end the war. Good for him! So I might not see him again
for a long time. Bad for me. For I knew now what my
answer was going to be. I missed him so much, I couldn't
stand thinking about it.

I closed my eyes and leaned back, and thought instead
about his belief that I had single-handedly changed my
life. He wasn't entirely correct. The first time, I'd gotten
help from Jonas the glassblower and from the coachman,
who undoubtedly undercharged me for driving me to the
castle gate. The second time, I never would have gotten
out of the dungeon without Mary bringing the shovel and
food. If I'd learned nothing else from the refugee camp, it
was that even the most independent people sometimes
needed help. And if I'd learned nothing else from my life
thus far, it was that you don't always end up where you
think you're going.

I smiled faintly, remembering the day I'd been swept
off to the castle. Everything had happened in such a blur
that my memories now were mostly just of scattered

sensations: the sound of the awestruck crowd whispering as they gathered around the prince's carriage, the feel of the silky dress the royal attendants put on me, the sight of the footman bowing low to me—to me!—before he helped me into the carriage. I couldn't have said now who was in the crowd, what color the dress was, or which hand the footman extended to me. Somehow only one detail still stood out clearly. I could still hear the voice of the old woman in my village, cackling as I rode by: "Now, there's one who will live happily ever after." And I remembered how fervently I had wanted to believe her, how I had looked out at her wrinkled, wizened face as if hoping to see the countenance of a prophet.

I was young. I could be excused my foolishness. But evidently the woman's advanced years had not earned her the wisdom she deserved. The last nine months of my life had hardly contained endless happiness, and I had little reason to expect endless happiness in the future. Why did the woman's prediction still haunt me?

I stood and walked to the window. Outside, children with ragged clothes, runny noses, and wind-chapped faces were playing a game they'd invented, throwing clods of frozen mud at the roof and laughing when smaller clumps of dirt rained back down on them. It was an ugly scene—certainly any of the women back in the castle would have sniffed in disgust and turned back to their fancy silks and satins, their perfect little needlepoint designs. But I saw the joy in the children's eyes, the jubilation on their faces every time a particularly big clod broke. I saw, well, beauty.

And suddenly I understood the old woman's prediction in a new light. Happiness was like beauty—in the eye of the beholder. Maybe the old woman could be right in a way she'd never intended. I did know this: I liked my life the way I was living it.

I turned from my window and went back to work.

her mantle. When friends asked her who the woman was, she could not answer. The woman I love, she wanted to say. But one day, in another year, she moved the picture behind a bunch of others on the coffee table in the new apartment she shared with Janie. And when someone happened upon it and asked her then, she said that it was just a friend.

Jen Michalski is author of the novel *The Tide King* (Black Lawrence press, 2013), winner of the 2012 Big Moose Prize, and the short story collections *From Here* and *Close Encounters*. She is the founding editor of the literary quarterly *jmww*, a co-host of The 510 Readings, and interviews writers at The Nervous Breakdown. She lives in Baltimore, MD, and tweets at www.twitter.com/ MichalskiJen. Find her at jenmichalski.com.